SPECIAL MESSAGE TO READERS

THE ULVERSCROFT FOUNDATION
(registered UK charity number 264873)

was established in 1972 to provide funds for research, diagnosis and treatment of eye diseases. Examples of major projects funded by the Ulverscroft Foundation are:-

- The Children's Eye Unit at Moorfields Eye Hospital, London
- The Ulverscroft Children's Eye Unit at Great Ormond Street Hospital for Sick Children
- Funding research into eye diseases and treatment at the Department of Ophthalmology, University of Leicester
- The Ulverscroft Vision Research Group, Institute of Child Health
- Twin operating theatres at the Western Ophthalmic Hospital, London
- The Chair of Ophthalmology at the Royal Australian College of Ophthalmologists

You can help further the work of the Foundation by making a donation or leaving a legacy. Every contribution is gratefully received. If you would like to help support the Foundation or require further information, please contact:

THE ULVERSCROFT FOUNDATION
The Green, Bradgate Road, Anstey
Leicester LE7 7FU, England
Tel: (0116) 236 4325

website: www.foundation.ulverscroft.com

THE SILVER LINING

Lady Stratton and her daughter Julia are living in straitened circumstances near the de Vere estate. When Gareth de Vere crashes his phaeton outside their cottage, he mistakes Julia for the maid. Although their attraction to each other grows with further encounters, their different social standings make it a mismatch. And despite a plot to provoke Gareth's feelings by his dissolute cousin, Fenton, Julia knows there is no chance of overcoming their circumstances — she is destined to love in vain . . .

Books by Wendy Kremer in the Linford Romance Library:

REAP THE WHIRLWIND
AT THE END OF THE RAINBOW
WHERE THE BLUEBELLS GROW WILD
WHEN WORDS GET IN THE WAY
COTTAGE IN THE COUNTRY
WAITING FOR A STAR TO FALL
SWINGS AND ROUNDABOUTS
KNAVE OF DIAMONDS
SPADES AND HEARTS
TAKING STEPS
I'LL BE WAITING
HEARTS AND CRAFTS
THE HEART SHALL CHOOSE
THE HOUSE OF RODRIGUEZ
WILD FRANGIPANI
TRUE COLOURS
A SUMMER IN TUSCANY
LOST AND FOUND
TOO GOOD TO BE TRUE
UNEASY ALLIANCE
IN PERFECT HARMONY
THE INHERITANCE
DISCOVERING LOVE
IT'S NEVER TOO LATE
THE MOST WONDERFUL TIME OF THE YEAR

WENDY KREMER

THE SILVER LINING

Complete and Unabridged

LINFORD
Leicester

First published in Great Britain in 2016

First Linford Edition
published 2018

A catalogue record for this book is available from the British Library.

ISBN 978–1–4448–3544–1

Published by
F. A. Thorpe (Publishing)
Anstey, Leicestershire

Set by Words & Graphics Ltd.
Anstey, Leicestershire
Printed and bound in Great Britain by
T. J. International Ltd., Padstow, Cornwall

This book is printed on acid-free paper

1

Lady Stratton went to throw some stale bread into the chicken coop at the back of the cottage. George was nearby, cleaning out the stables.

'Good morning George! It's a lovely morning.'

'Yes, ma'am, just the job. Are you looking for Miss Julia? She's working in the front garden.'

Lady Stratton frowned. 'Yes, I know. She will absolutely ruin her complexion and get calloused hands, but there's no stopping her. I always warned my husband it was wrong to let her grow up wild, like a boy. She and James were constant rivals for everything. Sir John was too indulgent. He insisted that his children must have a free and happy childhood without too many restraints.'

George laughed. 'If you'll forgive me saying so, ma'am, even though she's liberal and independent, they aren't bad qualities, are they? She's well-mannered, and anyone can tell that she's a lady.'

A tiny frown appeared again before she nodded. 'I suppose so. Well, I must get on. The vicar and Mrs Dutton are calling this evening.'

* * *

Julia had just tied up the hollyhocks. She loved the garden. It had demanded much of her time ever since they moved, but she'd grown to love the work. The garden was beginning look very pretty. She pushed her straw bonnet more tightly into place again and re-tied the brown ribbon in a tight side bow. Her cinnamon-coloured dress, with its high waist and long sleeves, had seen better days. She'd removed the decorative frills on the bottom of the skirt and the edges of the sleeves and added a useful side pocket. It looked very unassuming now, but at least the straight lines allowed her to move between plants and bushes without the material catching on something all the time. She tried to placate Mama by always dressing suitably when she was indoors; but when she worked outside, helped May with bottling or with drying the herbs, even Mama understood the practicalities of her wearing an old muslin dress like this one. Indoors with Mama, and especially on Sunday, she always wore something much prettier. Her mother was an accomplished needlewoman and wanted her daughter to shine down everyone else attending the church service.

Julia had had no personal maid before they moved, so their upheaval had made little difference as far as that was concerned. She managed her hair and all the rest very well without one.

She threw her arms around a bunch of tall blue lupines and tried to hold them together, to tie them with a strip of plaited straw. The sound of galloping horses distracted her and she loosened her grip for a second. The flowers fanned out again as she conjectured that there was a carriage as well as horses approaching; and whoever it was, they were in a hurry. As a rule, they only saw vehicles belonging to people who were acquainted with the back road to the village. Their red-brick cottage with its plain-tiled roof was off the road, but situated almost level with the bend. They had a good view in both directions, and Julia saw there was a large lumbering farm-cart approaching from the direction of the village. Bobby Grant was a gentle, empty-headed farmworker, and he was driving the cart dead centre. It had almost reached the corner when two black horses pulling a maroon phaeton flew past their garden gate. The ensuing gush of wind ruffled the curls escaping her straw bonnet.

Julia anticipated it before it happened. The driver of the phaeton couldn't check his horses in time. He was obviously skilled, and 'a swell of the first stare' as her brother James would have noted. He avoided a direct collision by a hazardous manoeuvre of guiding the four-wheeled carriage along the crest of a ditch. The horses protested loudly as they noticed the carriage was on hazardous ground and in danger of slipping. Their owner managed to bring the conveyance to an abrupt halt, but he lost his grip on the reins and was thrown from the high perch. The carriage shook, righted itself, and ended up tilting slightly inwards. Silence reigned for a moment before the stranger tried to get to his feet, but then fell back with a couple of colourful expressions Julia had last heard James using when he'd been spitting mad about something.

She smothered a laugh and watched the man grab the spoke of a wheel, then pull himself to rest against it. Bobby was busy trying to calm his frightened Welsh Cob. George came running from out back, and wordlessly Julia pointed down the road.

The phaeton's horses were slightly calmer now, but they were still dancing very nervously on the spot. Their harnesses jingled, they snorted, and their eyes rolled in fright. Their owner tried to pacify them from his sitting position with reassuring words.

Julia said, 'Help them, George. The horses might bolt if someone doesn't get them under control soon. Their owner is hurt. He tried to stand up a minute ago, but failed to do so.'

Bobby's cart was motionless, although the placid farm horse was treading from one big hoof to the other, uncertain what all the commotion was about. Bobby was shocked and scared, and the stranger was still talking in soft tones to his animals when George arrived. He bent and spoke briefly to the gentleman on the ground, who gestured him in the direction of his animals.

By now Julia's mother had joined her at the fence; and when she saw what had happened, she said, 'Oh dear! Is someone hurt?'

'Bobby's unharmed, but the other man took a tumble and he's hurt his leg or his foot. He can't stand properly. George is seeing to the horses first.

They could bolt.'

Her mother nodded. 'George has a way with animals. He'll have to stable them with Peggy out the back until someone comes to fetch them. Thoroughbreds are highly strung and nervous. I hope they won't eat all of Peggy's grain. It was expensive.'

They watched for a moment as George gradually appeased and unharnessed the team of horses. He exchanged a few words with the gentleman when he passed again, and the horses whinnied in recognition when they heard the man's voice. George returned to the cottage with two perfectly matched black stallions in tow. They tossed their heads, but followed him without too much protest.

George said, 'The gentleman has probably sprained or broken his ankle. He's clearly nobility. He didn't like me telling him to stay put, but he doesn't have much choice. I'll go back to help him as soon as I've settled the horses round the back. Peggy will have the shock of her life when she sees these fine steppers! I'll give them some water and leave them tied up outside. There's no chance of me stabling them with Peggy. They're too big for our boxes.'

Julia commented, 'You won't be able to move that carriage back safely on the road on your own; it leans too steeply. We can't help, and even with Bobby's help you won't manage it. It could easily topple over into the ditch. Someone will have to secure it with rope from the roadway while others push it back onto the hard surface again. You'll have to get someone from the village to help.'

Julia's mother nodded. 'He looks like a gentleman of the first *ton*, and the phaeton is quite beautiful. It has a coat of arms on the side and must have cost a fortune. Only nobility can afford such a carriage.'

Julia smiled to herself as she noticed how her mother had slipped back into the old habit of assessing people's standing by their possessions and looks. 'Bring him here, George, and then to go for Doctor Dunbar. Perhaps you can ask the smithy and some others to come back with you to deal with the carriage when you're there.'

Her mother turned and bustled off towards the cottage to prepare things for their unexpected visitor. Julia watched as Bobby jumped down from the driving seat and knelt down beside the stranger. He turned his cap nervously in his hands, looking extremely worried. Julia imagined just how Farmer Blake would react, and how he would bellow at Bobby if this man complained to him about his farmhand's stupidity. Bobby wasn't so foolish that he didn't know he was in big trouble if that happened. Seemingly the stranger had absorbed and digested his anger. He signalled that Bobby should be off, and with much sneaking, skulking and cap-raising Bobby did so, swiftly.

George returned to the scene just as Bobby began to drive away. He gestured towards the cottage and helped the man to his feet. The stranger protested and frowned, but George pulled him upright and he hobbled ham-fistedly towards their cottage, using George's arm as a support now and then. Julia hurried inside to see what her mother was doing.

She found her plumping the cushions on the stiff angular sofa in their main parlour. Julia liked the room; it was full of sunshine almost all afternoon until late evening. It had blue wallpaper with matching striped blue curtains. The furniture was sparse but of good quality: a Pembroke table, a stiff angular couch, a sideboard, some formal dining chairs, and a window seat with thick cushions. Julia spent a lot of time hunched up there, because it gave her plenty of light to read. It always reminded her of a similar window seat she'd had in her bedroom in her old home. There was also a polished pine armchair each side of the fireplace and the luxury of a small rectangular carpet they'd been allowed to bring with them to their new home. Above the sideboard was a long shelf holding a number of her father's favourite books, including one on gardening that had proved invaluable. Cousin Henry and his wife Georgina had been generous and allowed her to take them from the library when they moved.

Her mother looked up when she entered. 'Julia — get a pitcher of water from the stream. May has gone to the village. If the gentleman has sprained his ankle, cold water will lessen the swelling.' She looked in slight despair at her daughter's appearance. 'Oh dear! Why did this happen when you are wearing your very least becoming dress?'

Julia laughed softly. 'Mama, you know very well it doesn't make any difference anymore. Our necessity to act according to social standing ended with Papa's death. This gentleman, whoever he is, will pay no attention to anyone who is living in a cottage at the edge of a small village without sixpence to scratch with.' She rushed to add, 'And it doesn't matter; I don't mind, and you know so. We've talked about what has happened so often. I accept what fate has dealt us. I would give anything to have Papa and James with us again, but as that's impossible, I try to remember that we are still better off than many others. It makes no difference how I'm dressed — we are only doing a stranger a service because he happened to have an accident outside our door.'

Lady Stratton sighed and straightened her morning cap and the skirt of her neat dress. 'Yes, you're right. I miss your father sorely, and I still can't believe both he and James are dead. But I will never stop thinking that you were meant for better things.' She glanced out of the window. 'Oh, here's George with the gentleman on his arm. Off you go for some cold water!'

Julia did as she was told, and by the time she returned to the parlour it seemed full to overflowing, with George's bulky figure receiving last-minute instructions from Lady Stratton, and the unknown gentleman sitting upright on the sofa with one long leg set upon the carpet and the other hanging over its end. Julia noted his slim figure, suede buckskins, and that the shoeless foot wore a fine silk stocking. She'd listened to her brother's' detailed descriptions about clothes and tailors often enough to speculate that this man's coat was probably a creation by a master of his trade. It was of pure black fine wool with large pewter buttons. It fitted its owner like a second skin. She also noticed faultless small clothes and a pale grey silk embroidered waistcoat. He was dark, and his features were almost handsome. He paid her no attention when she poured the cold water into a bowl and put it on the floor.

Lady Stratton said, 'I think if you place your foot in the cold water it will help, my lord. I have sent my servant for the doctor. When they return, George will attend to you, and then we will send a message to your family. I expect they'll want to make arrangements to fetch you.'

He looked at her and nodded his acknowledgement. He had a hard, distinctive jawline. It was softened by a charming smile when he answered politely. 'I will be very obliged, if it is no trouble, Lady Stratton.'

'May I offer you a cup of tea, my lord? We can offer you some ratafia if you prefer, but I'm afraid we have nothing stronger.'

With a voice that indicated the best kind of education and society, he answered, 'A cup of tea would be most welcome, Lady Stratton. I must apologize for causing so much disruption.'

She gave him a brief curtsey. 'I declare it is no trouble. I'm sure George will return with the doctor directly, if he is at home.'

Julia followed her mother out of the door. When they were outside in the hallway, she remarked, 'He is very polite, isn't he — but he has traces of haughtiness about him.'

Looking at the closed door and whispering, Mama answered, 'He is entitled to be a little proud. He gave me his card. He is Marquess Gareth Cornelius de Vere. When I read his name, I remembered that your papa mentioned the de

Veres once or twice. The family can trace itself back to Norman times. They own extensive lands and properties in Northumberland and Devon, and have another estate near here.' She looked thoughtful. 'Papa met Marquess de Vere at meetings of the Society, and was impressed by his knowledge and gentlemanly conduct. He must have been this young man's father.'

'I wonder why he was driving past our cottage and not via the main road.'

Her mother shrugged. 'Why not? If he lives near here, he'd know of the shortcuts and back roads. When we first arrived, I remember the vicar mentioning they'd been invited to a picnic at Cobham Abbey. At the time I didn't note any names, and I wasn't curious enough to ask for more details later. I expect running the estate brings him here often.'

They went into the kitchen, and Julia helped to prepare a tray with their best china and a dish of small cakes that May had baked that morning. On their way back through the panelled hall, movement outside caught Julia's eye.

'Doctor Dunbar is coming up the path with George.'

'That's good. I will just deposit this tray and leave them. The doctor will want to examine his foot.'

Julia left her mother to return to the garden. She extracted a pair of cotton gloves from her side pocket and put them on. Her bonnet had been hanging loosely down her back. She tied it into place again and went back to her work in the garden.

The smell of fresh grass, the buzzing of the bees among the flowers, the song of birds somewhere in the bordering hedge, and the sweet perfume from the roses climbing the cottage wall lulled her into a feeling of wellbeing, and she went on tidying and trimming.

Doctor Dunbar stopped for a brief moment on his way out. Speaking quickly, he said, 'Afternoon Julia! Busy as ever, I see.'

She smiled at him. 'Yes, gardening

never ends, but I enjoy it. George helps with the heavy work.'

'My wife said those carrots you gave her are some of the best she's ever had.'

Julia pinked with pleasure. 'Really? That's very kind of her to say so! How is our patient?'

'He was lucky. It could have been a lot more serious, but it is only a bad strain. I've applied some of my liniment, bandaged it, and given him a pot to continue the treatment. He now seems to be extremely anxious to get home. He was just asking if your mother would allow George to drive him back to Cobham Abbey.'

Julia's eyes twinkled. 'What a comedown — setting forth in a phaeton and a pair of sweet goers, and returning in a second-hand pony-cart drawn by our Peggy!'

Dr Dunbar smiled. 'He seems to be a well-bred, civil kind of man. Somehow I don't think that bothers him as long as he achieves his objectives. I'd guess he dislikes fuss and wants to avoid commotion. He stated he doesn't mind how he gets there, as long as he doesn't have to walk. It's the first time I've ever treated a marquess. I must say, he's polite and more pleasant than I ever imagined nobility would be.'

'And why not? You're an excellent doctor, he needed your help, and you've helped him. He has every reason to be polite and pleasant.'

The doctor's cheeks bulged and he chuckled. 'In the course of my life, I've treated many people of much lower standing who were arrogant and often insolent.' He lifted his hat briefly. 'I must be off. Thomas Wilcox is not yet out of danger. It's still touch and go!'

Julia nodded. 'If there's anything I can do . . . '

He patted her arm. 'You're a good girl, Julia, but there's nothing anyone can do. Thomas has to fight this fight on his own, though I'll pass your message on to his wife.'

Julia watched him set off for the village. He'd walked to their cottage because harnessing his carriage for such a short distance wasn't worth the bother.

She heard the cottage door open and saw George hurrying round the corner. Her mother had clearly agreed to their guest's request, and George was off to harness their pony-cart.

A few minutes later, Marquess de Vere dipped his head as he exited their arched doorway. He was leaning heavily on a silver-topped walking stick that Julia recognized as one that had belonged to her father. There was not a hair on his head out of place. He could have just been about to enter a fashionable soirée instead of returning unexpectedly home after a coaching accident. Julia had time to study him more closely because he was paying attention to how to use the stick effectively. His sprained foot was bandaged and looked bulky in his shoe, but he managed. She noted he didn't follow the fashion of powdering his hair. It was drawn back and tied in a short dark bunch with a black ribbon. His features were ascetic, his eyes dark and inquisitive, his nose thin and slightly out of line. His figure was slender, and it was clear that he either participated in sport of some kind or spent a great deal of time outdoors. He looked up and caught her eye for a moment. Julia blushed and looked away quickly.

The marquess did his best to speedily negotiate the winding stone pathway, but he had to take care, as it was uneven. By the time he'd managed the greater part, George was already bringing their pony-cart to the front. When Lord de Vere reached the gate, he turned and beckoned to Julia. Startled, and reacting instinctively, she came across to where he stood. The marquess viewed her. She was a pretty maid, delicate, slightly above average height, with dark hair, fine skin, and sparkling dark eyes. She looked at him and fiddled with a length of plaited straw in her gloved hands.

He fished in the pocket of his waistcoat and handed her a silver coin. 'Thank you for procuring the cold water! It helped prodigiously.' He turned away and resumed his way to the waiting vehicle.

She was caught completely off guard and remained speechless. He failed to notice her astonishment, and George could only blink rapidly at the scene.

He thought she was a servant! Julia fingered the half crown. She chuckled softly and thought about advising him of his mistake, but decided not to bother. He was already climbing into the pony-cart with George's help. Julia gesticulated for George's attention and put her finger to her mouth. She'd never see the marquess again and she couldn't blame him for mistaking her for a housemaid. They hadn't been properly introduced, and she was dressed like a servant. Well, let him believe what he liked. She pocketed the coin and decided it would be useful to help pay her annual fee at the lending library in the next town. Her godmother had paid her entrance fee, but the annual fee was her sole concern.

* * *

George set off at a steady pace. The man sitting next to him had rank, wealth, elegance and a quick tongue, but he also seemed to be just and rational. He hadn't insisted on blaming Bobby, he'd shunned unnecessary fuss, and he expected no toadying from anyone.

'You'll give me timely directions, my lord? Our Peggy isn't comparable to your pair; sometimes she acts bird-witted if you don't give her due warning.'

Glad to be no longer at the centre of the care and attention of the doctor and Lady Stratton, Gareth looked down at the back of the roan pony pulling them along. 'Horses are like people. They have their own characters. Just follow this road and then branch off at the Pig and Whistle. You'll see the entrance to

Cobham about two miles further down that road.'

Gareth tested his foot on the carriage floor and was satisfied. The pain had lessened considerably already.

'I don't think your carriage is mulled up too much, sir, but perhaps it would be sensible to get it checked before someone fetches it? The main body has a couple of scratches, but some vigorous polishing will remove them. If there is any damage, it will be to the wheels. Will you allow me to let our local smithy take a look? He's not a wheelwright, but he can tell if something is damaged or loose.'

'Yes, do that by all means. I'm grateful, George. I think that's your name, isn't it? Without your help, and that of Lady Stratton, I'd be in a pickle.'

George flicked the reins and Peggy obligingly picked up speed. 'Don't mention it, my lord. I know Lady Stratton and her daughter were pleased to help.'

Eyeing the passing countryside, and testing pressure on his sprained foot on the floor of the cart again, Gareth said, 'I gather that Lady Stratton is a widow?'

'Yes, sir. Lady Stratton's son was killed in a hunting accident nearly two years ago, and a year later sir James caught a severe cold that spread to his lungs and left the ladies fairly destitute. The family used to own a small, prosperous estate the other side of Axminster. It wasn't big, roughly a thousand acres, but it provided them with a decent income and they were good employers. The problems started when Mr James, the son, was killed. The estate was entailed, and even though Sir John tried to arrange things so that the two ladies wouldn't be quite destitute on the occasion of his death, he didn't have time enough to complete all his plans. But who expected that he would pass on so quickly after his son? Luckily he'd arranged the purchase of the cottage. It's in range of the manor house, but far enough away to avoid distress. Sir John's secretary told me he'd planned to endow his daughter, and negotiations were well advanced, but then he took very ill. The estate went to some distant cousin and the two women had to leave.'

Gareth looked thoughtful. 'I've seen it occur often. The head of a family should make sure it doesn't happen. Lady Stratton seems like a very nice, genteel lady.'

'She is, sir. She is kind and understanding. She was just the same, even when she ran a large house and had several servants. Now there's just my wife, and myself. We could have stayed with the new owners, or looked for another position like all the others did, but May and I talked about it and we decided to stay with Lady Stratton. She was good to us, she pays a fair wage, and we like country life.'

'I'm sure that they are grateful. You live in the house?'

'Yes, sir. We have a couple of rooms at the back. May does the cooking and helps with the housework. Another girl comes help with cleaning once a week. I do any heavy work — repairs, looking after the pony, digging in the garden, looking after the chickens.'

'May is your wife?' Gareth reflected that from the brief glance he'd had, George must be a lot older than her.

George nodded. 'Yes, sir. She was in the village fetching some flour and other groceries when your mishap occurred.'

Gareth was puzzled. 'But the girl? The one who brought the water, the one in the garden just now? She was the help from the village?'

George laughed. 'Lord no, sir! That was Miss Julia, Lady Stratton's daughter.'

Gareth recalled shoving the coin into her gloved hand and tried not to frown. He drew his head back stiffly and pulled at the collar of his necktie. 'But she looked like a country maid.'

George laughed. 'Yes, Lady Stratton gets puffed up by how she dresses; but Miss Julia has a mind of her own, and to be perfectly honest if you work in the garden there isn't much point in dressing in your best clothes, is there?'

Busy guiding the pony-cart down the side lane bordering the Pig and Whistle, George didn't notice how his passenger pressed his lips tightly together and how his face took on an uneasy expression.

Gareth stared unseeingly at the passing countryside and felt annoyed. The girl must have thought him an arrogant idiot, or simply jiggle-brained. Admittedly he had been going a tad too fast on that stretch of road, and unfortunately the other driver was slow-witted. He hadn't kicked up a rumpus because the lad would have received the sharp end of his employer's tongue. He wasn't his employee, so there was no reason to torment him. Any scratches on the phaeton would annoy his stable hands, but they all knew better than to question him too closely. What a morning! And he still had to face the consoling observations of the family. He could at least look forward to playing billiards or chess with Hugh after dinner. His brother-in-law didn't play chess, and the cleric spoiled the game by his perpetual sycophantic remarks.

What bad luck that the two vehicles had met just then, just there, this afternoon. On top of that, he'd mistakenly identified the daughter for a common maid. It was vexing, and a damned nuisance too. Civility demanded he'd have to make some kind of suitable apology and reparation.

When they reached Cobham, he slipped George a guinea and arranged with the head groom to see about the recovery of the phaeton and the horses straight away. Orders given, and the afternoon now well advanced, Gareth took his chance to slip indoors unseen.

2

In her bedroom, Julia washed and changed into a pale pink morning dress of fine cotton with a high waist and long sleeves ending in points. Pink wasn't her favourite colour, but she had to admit it suited her dark brown hair and brown eyes. In her latest letter, her aunt had written that blondes were all the rage in London at the moment, so when she visited them she wouldn't attract many admirers. Not that she wanted to anyway. She thought her looks were passable; her best features were her skin and her almond-shaped eyes. She sighed as she viewed herself in the toilet mirror. She took a necklace of seed pearls out of the drawer at its base. There! She was decent enough for even the Marquess de Vere. He wouldn't admire, but she was presentable enough to earn his approval.

She glanced at the plain wooden table in front of the window, which she employed as a writing desk. There were some empty foolscaps of paper lying there, next to a full inkwell. She deliberately hadn't mentioned the marquess's slip-up to her mother because Mama was too charmed by their visitor, and Julia didn't want to destroy any illusions she'd formed. After tea she'd write to Amelia and tell her all about it. Normally little happened in the village worth reporting: her gardening, her attempts to lessen the hardships of some of the villagers, their visits to the vicarage, the return suppers at their cottage, and their occasional trip to the next town where Julia haunted the lending library.

Amelia had more exciting meetings and outings to report. Julia wondered if she sometimes deliberately moderated the tone of her letters so that they wouldn't make her feel envious. Julia was grateful to have such a loyal friend. They'd shared their schooling, grown up together, and remained close. Julia had secretly hoped that Amelia and James would marry. Perhaps the two sets of parents had hoped the same so that the neighbouring estates would be joined, but that was not to be. Now the two girls lived apart, and their contact was limited to letters and occasional visits.

Julia glanced out of her window across the vegetable garden to the meadows beyond. She picked up a paisley shawl from the back of a Windsor armchair and arranged it gracefully round her shoulders before she joined her mother for their little daily luxury of afternoon tea in the parlour.

* * *

As Gareth made his way through the vast candle-lit main hall towards the dining room, he was reminded yet again that his inheritance was not a plaything, and it was his destined job in life to maintain and uphold his legacy for the next generation. All of the property and possessions belonged to him at present, but it was his only on loan.

His mother, sister, brother-in-law and a few other guests were on a short visit. Recently his mother had announced she wanted to settle in the Dower House at Cobham. She knew a great deal about running the estate here, and as he was not married, she could help to keep an eye on the place for him and leave him more time to manage the others. He knew it would be to his advantage if she lived here permanently.

He glanced at the rooms he passed through on the way to the small dining room. The housekeeper in Cobham kept high standards, even though there was no mistress to please. She was strict. She reminded the other servants of their duties constantly, and that they were to perform them with dignity. Their jobs were well-paid, and they were sought-after positions. The men wore blue and gold livery and the female servants wore black gowns with stiffly starched pin-afores and mobcaps. Thomas the butler kept an eagle eye on proceedings, and was in charge of the decanters containing the various spirits and wines that circled the table during the meals. Between the courses the other servants withdrew, but Thomas remained in the background, discretely monitoring the meal. In the same way, he discreetly managed and controlled most of the happenings in and outside Cobham. Only the marquess's valet carried more voice in the house.

There was a deep blue sky fading into the colours of evening visible through the long paned windows. They were framed on each side with heavy rich brocade drapes. The dining table looked elegant, with crystal glasses, old silver and costly porcelain, all ready and waiting on the starched white tablecloth. The servants knew the marquess would complain in no short terms if he thought standards were slacking. He also knew that good service was vital to the smooth running of his estates. He treated his employees fairly and paid them well.

He looked at his fob watch and nodded to the butler as he entered the long dining room. Gareth was glad he'd been able to escape most of the questioning about what had happened earlier with the excuse he had to change for the evening meal. He joined the others without a noticeable limp and took his place at the head of the table. He managed to mask the slight discomfort he felt splendidly. His valet had bandaged his foot tightly and applied some more of the good doctor's ointment. He wore evening shoes that shone from expert polishing but were well worn. Much to his valet's chagrin, he did without his usual elegant narrow footwear this evening, but felt a lot more comfortable for doing so.

Gareth's sister Caroline sat to his left; his mother, Lady de Vere, to his right. Caroline's husband and his friend Hugh faced each other across the table next to them. The men eyed him sympathetically and lifted their brows as the women began to question him about his mishap. Further down the long table were Caroline's friend, Charlotte Dandridge; Colonel and Mrs Weston; his mother's companion, their permanent cleric, Dr Jameson; and a local magistrate who had been invited to share the meal. They all listened with interest to the conversation as they spooned their clear soup, especially the family cleric. Cobham had a private chapel, and the family attended regularly when they resided. The servants were expected to attend if they didn't have the day off. As that rarely happened, the parson was sure that he would not preach his sermon to empty pews, and he was aware that God had provided him with a post that many of his fellow clergy envied.

If in residence at Cobham, Gareth generally attended Sunday service at his old tutor's church. William had been married and settled in the parsonage at Witheringston for many years. He'd offered William, his old tutor, the post at Cobham Abbey when Gareth succeeded to the title. William had never been a toad-eater and insisted he was comfortable enough where he was. He added that it would always give him immense pleasure to see his lordship whenever he was in the vicinity and had time to call. Gareth had been on his way there this afternoon when the mishap happened.

When Gareth was little, Dr William Dunbar had been a mere young parish-incumbent and unmarried. His father heard of him, his high education and his good character. William was offered, and took, the post of tutor to the heir of the de Vere estates, and travelled with him and the rest of the family wherever they went. He taught Gareth and helped him to become aware of, and accept, his future responsibilities. He also provided the intelligent young man with standards of learning that enabled him to get through university with above-average results, and the necessary polish and decorum that had smoothed his way through society ever since. Gareth sometimes thought he was closer to William than to most of his own family, and especially since his father's death. He could always turn to William for an honest opinion and unbiased advice.

He held up his hand, and the white of his wide pleated wristband flashed below the sleeve of his black evening coat for a second. 'Caro, I wish you to change the subject; this one is boring. My foot is already much better. The village doctor plastered it with an ointment that is doing its job splendidly.'

The silk of her evening gown rustled as Caroline moved uneasily in her chair. Her hands fluttered and gestured as she went on. 'You could have been killed, Gareth! How can you ignore the possibility and pretend that it was a trivial event?'

Gareth hid his irritation. His eyes were hooded and he concentrated on the removal of the soup-plate by one of the servants and watching how a gold-edged empty one was placed on the same spot. He helped himself to a slice of wild pork from a silver platter carried by a servant and some potatoes from another. He waved away the rest. Everyone else began to fill their plates, and there was a clapper of silver for a few moments until the servants withdrew.

Lady de Vere shook her head covertly at her daughter; an indication that she should not continue to censure her brother. She knew it was pointless to try to force him, but she also knew it was a chance to seize a rare opportunity to repeat what was close to her heart, something that was growing more important with every passing year. 'I understand Caroline's fears completely, Gareth, and I must remind you that until you marry and sire an heir, Felton is your legal heir. Yet he is a spendthrift and a scoundrel. His reputation is nil, his debts are reputed to be gigantic, and they will drain the estate before the ink is dried on the paper — if he inherits.'

Gareth's lips thinned. His mother

had a rare gift of always choosing the wrong moment to remind him of his responsibilities. She'd been marchioness too long to ever forget her duty. She loved him in her own way, but the title and all it stood for would always be foremost in her mind. She'd already mentioned the same thing several times in recent months.

'I am fully aware of Felton's reputation, Mother. I am also fully aware of my duties. I know what is expected of me. I fully intend to give due attention to your suggestion at an opportune time.'

His mother nodded gratefully. 'Then I am reassured.'

'I promise you that I will make every effort to thwart any plans that my cousin Felton may be hatching to inherit my title.' His plate was empty and he threw his napkin on the table. 'I have no more appetite this evening, but pray continue with the rest of the meal without me.'

The gathering looked down at their plates or at each other before busying themselves with the remaining courses. Thomas hurried to open the door that enabled the marquess a fluid departure.

Gareth made his way to the library, where a bright fire was burning despite the time of year. The room was on the side of the house that saw little sunshine. Sometimes when he entered it he noticed there was a slight mustiness in the air. One of his future plans for this house was to relocate the library to the other side, where sunshine helped to heat the rooms. His black evening tail-coat brushed a side table as he went towards the fire and rested his sprained foot in its shiny evening shoe on the fender. It didn't hurt half as much as it had earlier on, and whatever the doctor had mixed into that liniment, it was damned good.

Staring into the flickering flames, he wondered briefly what it would be like to have no responsibilities. Hugh was his best friend — had been since university days; and although Hugh only had a trifling income in comparison to his own, he often envied him. Hugh wasn't caged in by the responsibilities and the demands of a title, or what that title and inheritance entailed. Luckily Gareth had learned early on to control his emotions. Personal needs and wishes were secondary. It was easier to appear uncaring than to admit that one was as vulnerable as the next man. He noticed that people didn't bother him with trifling difficulties because they feared the sharp edge of his tongue. Few people knew him well. Hugh was one, William was another, and he had been close to his father too when he was still alive.

The flames flickered as he thought about his mother's words. She was right; it was time that he secured the line. Several seasons had come and gone and many debutantes had cried in frustration at his lack of interest. He recalled with distaste how they and their mothers had tried to tempt him. He hit the mantelpiece with the palm of his hand. Damn it! Still, if he set his mind to it, he'd soon find someone suitable to take his fancy for a short time until the title was safe. Arranged marriages were all the rage among some of his contemporaries. He'd never established if his own parents felt more for each other than duty demanded.

Up until now, an occasional affair had served to provide him with the kind of female company he needed. He had thought about installing an official mistress at a discreet address somewhere in London, but that was not to his taste. There were enough women of his acquaintance who were only too obliging if they were married to a boring, uncaring husband. He'd accept facts, examine the possibilities, find someone who wasn't a gabster and didn't bore him to tears, and make an offer.

He turned away from the fire abruptly and poured himself a glass of cognac from a decanter standing on a nearby table. His thoughts were still wandering, and he remembered his faux pas with Lady Stratton's daughter. He'd have to rectify that. A short, clear apology should suffice. He took his first sip of the golden liquid and it coated his throat with some welcome fire.

The door opened and Hugh came in. Gareth gave him one of his rare smiles. His friend wandered across, helped himself to a glass and lifted it in Gareth's direction. 'Hard luck, old chap. The women were sticking their pins in tonight, weren't they? If you'd pitched a gammon when you came back and just said you'd twisted your foot while you were out, you might have got away with it. When you turned up in that pony-cart, and you warned the stable hands the phaeton might be scratched, there was nothing more you could do to stop the gossip.'

He nodded. 'I know. I should have thought of the consequences, but I forgot how quickly they'd natter. Sometimes I have the feeling that if I relieved myself once too often during the day, someone would undoubtedly send for the quack.' Hugh laughed. 'Believe me, being a marquess with no brothers is strenuous work, my friend.'

'Ah, it does have benefits. You can afford anything and everything. You can get foxed whenever you like; and even when you are bosky, people will still do your bidding. They will jump in the lake at three in the morning if you tell them to do so.'

Gareth yawned artificially. 'I know; that's why it fags me to death sometimes. Where are the others?'

'The women are in the drawing room and the men have gone to the billiard room. I thought you might prefer a game of chess or just a chinwag. Am I right?'

Gareth clapped him on the shoulder. 'Completely! I must tell you something that the others shouldn't hear. I made a complete fool of myself this afternoon, and I have to make amends.'

Hugh tilted his head and lifted his brow. 'You? In a hobble? How come? How interesting! Fire ahead!'

Gareth looked across at his friend and thanked heaven. He was someone on whom he could rely on, no matter how silly or sticky the situation was. Hugh didn't gossip, never flattered him, and was always totally honest.

Hugh could tell Gareth was ill at ease this evening. He guessed that it had to do with his mother's reminder that he had no option but to marry, and as soon as possible. He couldn't recall Gareth ever being really in love with anyone. Not with one of errant wives or even one of the actresses who constantly hoped to catch his attention, and sometimes did. There'd been flirts and affairs, but no one had held his interest for long. If he was forced to marry, Hugh wasn't sure who he should feel sorrier for — Gareth, or the woman he was duty-bound to marry.

3

Hugh reluctantly agreed to accompany him a week later when the marquess announced he intended to call at the cottage to express his regret about his mistake, on his way to visit William at the vicarage.

By chance, Lady Stratton saw them drawing up outside and called upstairs to Julia. 'My dear, straighten your hair. Marquess de Vere is at the gate with another gentleman.' She hurried back to the parlour, tidied her cap, arranged her dress, and picked up her needlework.

Minutes later May announced the visitors. 'Marquess de Vere and Mr Hugh Grenville, ma'am!'

Lady Stratton put the needlework aside and rose to her feet. She gave them a brief curtsey.

'Good afternoon, ma'am!' greeted

Gareth. 'I hope I am not intruding by calling unannounced like this. I wanted to return your walking stick and express my thanks for the way you helped me last week.' He offered her a small posy of summer flowers.

Lady Stratton smiled and accepted the flowers. 'It is very kind of you, your lordship, and quite unnecessary. I am glad to see you are restored again. We were pleased to help. Please take a seat!'

Gareth turned to his friend. 'Lady Stratton, this is my friend Hugh Grenville. I persuaded him to come with me because he needed exercise — he spends too much time indoors reading.'

Hugh stepped forward and extended his hand. 'Good afternoon, Lady Stratton. I'm pleased to meet you. I believe his lordship borrowed this walking stick?'

She took it and said, 'How do you do, sir. You are most welcome too. Please make yourself comfortable.'

Hugh was an easier conversationalist than his friend because he didn't need to adopt Gareth's haughtiness. But he appreciated why Gareth was so. There were too many grovelers and two-faced individuals who tried to claim Gareth's attention for their own purposes. He forestalled most of them by appearing wholly disinterested.

Hugh remarked, 'You have a very pretty cottage, Lady Stratton, and your front garden is a riot of colour.'

'Ah, that is due to the efforts of my daughter, Julia. She spends much time there, and seems to have green fingers.'

Lady Stratton sat and admired the men's attire. Both were dressed elegantly in square-cut tailcoats and polished boots. Both had high-collared white shirts and intricately tied neck-cloths. If anything, Marquess de Vere looked slightly the more elegant of the two, because his dark blue tailcoat was cut superbly and complemented by an embroidered pale grey silk waistcoat. He was also the taller of the two. Mr Grenville wore a bottle-green tailcoat with a double row of metal buttons. His neck-cloth spilled at the neck like a waterfall, and they both wore pale beige pantaloons.

The two men had barely settled when they were obliged to rise again as Julia entered. She eyed the two men and gave them a straight-backed curtsey. They responded with brief bows. Julia held his lordship's glance for a moment longer than Hugh's. With a slight feeling of discomfort, Gareth saw a hint of amusement in her eyes.

'His lordship has come to thank us for our help and has brought me some flowers.'

Julia nodded. Her colour was high. Hugh had expected to confront a chubby milkmaid, but Miss Stratton had delicate features, was slender, and more than just pretty.

Julia said, 'That is very considerate of his lordship, but I'm sure you've told him we expect no thanks.'

'I have.'

The marquess did not respond, so Julia turned her attention to Hugh. 'Doctor Dunbar's liniment seems to work wonders with breaks and sprains.

It is very famous hereabouts.'

Hugh gave her a soft smile. 'It does seem to have special healing properties. His lordship recovered very fast.' He lifted his brow. 'He also told me he thought the cold water you fetched helped to prevent further discomfort.'

Julia coloured slightly, and guessed that the marquess must have mentioned his unintentional blunder to his friend. He sat silently watching them, and his chance for adding an appropriate word passed. She said, 'If that is so, then I am glad.' She wondered why he was so unresponsive. Perhaps he thought it made him more worthy of note.

Suddenly he did express himself, and managed to sound disapproving as he did so. With narrowed eyes he declared, 'Your mother just mentioned that you manage the garden. It is hard to imagine why you enjoy messing around in the dirt and grime. It is an unusual task for a lady, isn't it?'

Looking past him at the row of books on the shelf above his head, she raised her eyebrows and stared ahead. 'I agree with you, my lord — it is unusual. But isn't there an appropriate saying going back to the times of the Peasant Riots that says, 'When Adam delved and Eve span, who was then the gentleman'? I can imagine why you find it hard to understand, but I actually enjoy messing about in the dirt and grime.' Julia touched the side of her muslin dress. 'And I don't garden in such things as this. I keep my clothes as simple as possible and could easily be mistaken for a kitchen maid.' Her mother looked at her disapprovingly. 'My mother despairs of me, and doesn't approve of me gardening, but it gives me great pleasure.'

Hugh had the urge to chuckle, and the corner of Gareth's mouth turned up for a second before he bent forward to brush off an imaginary piece of fluff. He guessed that the girl hadn't mentioned his faux pas to her mother, so he was off the hook. He wondered why. Most young ladies would delight in the chance to broadcast such an occurrence.

Lady Stratton hurried to ask, 'May I offer you some tea, my lord — Mr Grenville?'

The marquess stood up and proceeded to put on his gloves. 'It is most kind of you, Lady Stratton, but I am afraid I must decline. I've promised to call at the vicarage this afternoon, and I think Mrs Dutton will be expecting us to drink tea with them.'

Julia's mother nodded. 'I understand perfectly, sir. Please remember us to the vicar and his wife. They are both good people, and he is well loved by all his parishioners. Folk who have lived in the district much longer than we have tell me they've never had a kinder or more caring vicar.'

The marquess inclined his head. 'I can believe that, ma'am.'

Hugh didn't want to leave so easily. 'Perhaps Miss Stratton can give me a quick tour of her vegetable plot before we depart? I don't think I have ever seen one.'

Gareth remained stoically silent and

impassive. He extracted his fob watch and then said, 'I didn't know you were interested in vegetables, Hugh! If I had, I would have arranged a tour of the kitchen garden at Cobham. I'm sure that would provide you with a never-ending source of interest. You should have mentioned it before this.'

Hugh's eyes twinkled, and with tongue in cheek he said, 'Ah! But here I have chance to see things on a much smaller scale and learn about them from someone who is personally involved. Normally I only ever see vegetables on silver platters.'

The marquess gave him one of his rare smiles, and Julia was almost sorry she'd tried to counter his remarks about her gardening.

'If you are determined to see Miss Stratton's vegetables, by all means — but just for ten minutes, and then we must be off.' He gestured to the door. 'Lead the way, Miss Stratton!'

Julia went, followed by her mother. There was a bustle as they all crossed the hall and went outside. Julia walked ahead and rounded the corner of the cottage. She led Hugh along a crazy pavement and past a stretch of lawn to the back of the garden.

Lady Stratton waited with the marquess near the corner of the house and chatted about the vicar and his work in the village. Gareth nodded absentmindedly and added a comment at the appropriate moment when she mentioned something he knew. He wondered why he suddenly wished he'd shown as much interest as Hugh. Probably because Julia was pretty, and had a great deal of backbone and strength. From what their servant had told him on his trip home last week, her circumstances and prospects were less than rosy. She knew that too, and could have withdrawn into a comfortable shell and abandoned the drudgery to their remaining servants. But she hadn't. She knew it was beneath her social standing to do more than deadhead the roses, but she saw gardening as a way of helping to support them financially, and she didn't mind getting her hands dirty in the process. She even seemed to enjoy it.

Her soft laughter drifted across to him as she preceded Hugh along some orderly trenches. She stopped now and then to point something out, or when he asked a question. It was highly probable that Hugh had never seen vegetables actually growing in the ground before, but he had never wanted to fill that gap in his knowledge either — until today when he'd met Miss Stratton.

Now that she was dressed fittingly, the marquess admitted she had a good figure. He knew enough about female fashion to recognize that she was wearing a fashionable muslin morning dress. It was fastened in the back with small buttons and a buckle. Her dark hair was parted in the front, with full curls on each side. The whole picture was one of simple elegance, and the dress accentuated the girl's good posture and bearing. If it was an example of her taste, then it was a shame she would never move in the kind of circles she deserved to. Too many women of his acquaintance wore styles that had been recommended by their seamstress but were completely unsuitable. Too many dresses were intentionally made to catch the eye with too many frills, sashes, bows, flounces and other decorations.

She looked in their direction and met his glance for a moment. Admittedly she was attractive, and he couldn't imagine why he'd made the mistake of thinking that she was a household servant. She had too much poise and confidence for anyone to mistake her for anything but a lady. But it wasn't his habit to study servants too closely, and he had never met a lady who dressed like a servant before either. Julia looked away and began talking to his friend again about something else.

A few minutes later, the two men took their leave at the gate. Lady Stratton and Julia bobbed their thanks and said goodbye. They watched the carriage bowl round the corner on its way to the vicarage, then returned indoors. Lady Stratton arranged the marquess's flowers in a suitable container and stood it on the side table.

'That remark you made about Adam and Eve was quite unnecessary, Julia. What will the marquess think of us? He'll believe we are turning into rebels, because our means are so reduced.'

Julia kissed her cheek. 'He won't give it a second thought, Mama. He knows exactly what I meant.'

Lady Stratton nodded and went back to her needlework. She was pleased that she would be able to talk about the marquess's visit when they next met the vicar and his wife. She genuinely enjoyed their company.

Julia went upstairs, back to her letter writing. She'd been busy writing to her aunt and uncle in London when the visitors arrived. She deliberated that Hugh Grenville was a pleasant gentleman. No airs and graces, and willing to share a joke. Marquess de Vere was a completely different kettle of fish. She swallowed her laughter and wondered if she intentionally hoped to find fault with him. She hadn't made up her mind if he was an agreeable man or not. She hadn't exchanged a single personal word with him, and neither of them had referred to his gift of the half crown. He probably never would now. Biting on the shaft of the pen, she looked pensively out of the window for a moment before finally dipping it in the inkwell and filling a page with all the recent news.

⋆ ⋆ ⋆

The two friends were silent for a moment after they set off. Gareth was driving the curricle with his favourite team of dappled horses through the village towards the vicarage on the other side of the river. The clear waters of the stream flowed through the middle of the hamlet. The two parts of the village were connected via an ancient stonework bridge. Hugh viewed the main street, with its handful of shops and some busy pedestrians who were about their business as they passed.

When they were on the far side, Gareth said, 'You seemed very taken with Miss Stratton.'

His friend looked across and patted his top hat. 'She's bang up to the mark — well-read, with a delightful sense of humour. She has no airs and graces either, and she managed to put you in your place without giving you away. I have a feeling she never mentioned what happened, otherwise she or her mother would have referred to it.'

Gareth looked ahead. 'Yes, I believe you are right. She has overlooked it, and so will I. She is no light-skirt, Hugh, so don't get any wrong ideas. She's had a decent upbringing, and if things had gone right for her she would have ended up the wife of a country gentleman. As it is, she isn't likely to see much life beyond this village.'

Hugh nodded. 'She already told me

as much in so many words just now. Anyway, I don't think she's a female who can be led astray easily. She has too much backbone for that. I wasn't thinking of doing so anyway!' Sounding slightly indignant, he continued, 'I hope I am too much of a gentleman to try to take advantage of any woman in that kind of position. She's a likeable woman, I admit, even if we never meet again.'

De Vere grinned at his friend. 'You have a romantic soul, my friend. I think you would be perfect in the role of a knight in shining armour.'

* * *

The following Sunday, as was customary, Julia and her mother attended church. It was an opportunity to meet some of the other families from the village, and gradually the widow and her daughter were recognized and accepted faces in the community.

For some time now, Julia had taken it upon herself to visit a row of houses on the far side of the village where several families lived in utmost poverty. Some men had lost their jobs, there were three deserted wives left to care for their small children, and an old couple who lived in the end house. Most of them hoped something or someone would improve their lot before they'd pawned the last of their possessions and were left at the mercy of some unwilling relative or the harshness of the local poorhouse. Two widows took in washing, and another helped in the kitchen at the local inn, but they barely made ends meet. The old couple had children who had married and moved away. Their parents were dependent on the occasional shilling they received from them. It was barely enough to live decently in their old age, but they were the most cheerful ones whenever Julia called.

She had chanced on the run-down cottages while out walking, and the sight of small children playing unconcernedly close to the open drain had brought her back several times to try to relieve some of their wants. She came with a basket of spare vegetables, loaves of bread, or some badly needed cough mixture or ointment. At the moment she was trying to tactfully persuade the idle men to cover the drain and tidy the place up generally. It was an uphill fight. One or two of them openly resented her visits, and were bitter whenever she suggested any improvements. She knew they resented that she was telling them what to do, not only because she was a female, but also because she was a gentlewoman. Behind her back, they grumbled that the likes of her had no idea about what life meant for the likes of them.

Dr Dutton soon heard about her visits, and he praised her charitable ways whenever he got the chance. Julia's mother was not so happy about it, however; she worried constantly that her daughter would pick up some kind of life-threatening illness.

* * *

Julia and her mother took their place next to the vicar's wife, Maria Dutton. She and Lady Stratton got on well and even found they had some mutual friends. Just before the service began, there was a slight stir and people shifted in their seats as Marquess de Vere and Mr Grenville walked down the aisle to sit in their designated places at the front. The marquess looked straight ahead. Mr Grenville spotted them as they passed and nodded. Julia smiled back.

William Dutton's services were never boring, and his parishioners were hearty singers, so the time passed quickly and they were all soon trundling back outside the old church to head home again. Julia and her mother had already shaken hands with the vicar and were taking leave of his wife when Hugh Grenville joined them. De Vere was still talking to the vicar near the church porch-way.

He tipped his hat. 'This is an unexpected pleasure.'

Julia felt quite comfortable in his company. 'Good morning, Mr Grenville!

I didn't expect to see you here this morning.'

He smiled. 'Whenever I'm visiting, I come to church here with Gareth.' Looking at the vicar's wife, he explained briefly, 'The majority of clergymen think it is their duty to preach hell and damnation every week. Your husband, Mrs Dutton, makes us aware of our sins and our failings, but he encourages us to repent, and he also reassures us that our God is a very forgiving and lenient master.'

Maria Dutton laughed softly. 'Yes, William is not in favour of all the fire and brimstone you hear in most churches. He says no one wants to be told they are likely to end up in eternal hell when this life is over. Some people on the parish council have tried to change him and suggest his sermons should be more ominous and threatening, but they'll never succeed. His parishioners are very loyal and the church is always full. I think the council knows it would face a great deal of opposition if they tried to interfere in how or what he says or does.'

Hugh laughed. 'That says a lot about his character.' He looked up and noticed the vicar approaching with the marquess, who dipped his head and touched the rim of his hat.

Dr Dutton said, 'My dear, Gareth has invited us to attend a picnic at Cobham Abbey on Thursday. Are we free? Remember how delightful it was last year. It was such a beautiful day, wasn't it?'

Maria Dutton knew better than to refuse such an invitation. 'No, we have nothing special planned for Thursday.'

'Good, good!' The vicar clapped his hands behind his back, on the folds of his white surplice, and viewed the party genially.

Julia was surprised when the marquess added in a neutral tone, 'It would be pleasing if you and your daughter would come to too, Lady Stratton.'

Lady Stratton was flustered but she did as expected. 'Thank you for the invitation, my lord. We will be pleased to come.'

He nodded. 'Good. I'll send the

barouche to fetch you all. Two o'clock on Thursday? Apparently the cook is anxious to demonstrate her skills to a wider audience. It will not be a large party. Just the family and a few friends who are staying at the moment.' He turned to Julia. She was gowned modestly in a blue carriage dress with the minimum of decoration and a poke bonnet with a few flowers and a pale blue ribbon tied on one side in a bow. He acknowledged that she was a woman who could compel attention without employing the use of exaggerated fashion. 'I hope you are well?'

Julia felt her colour rise slightly. 'Thank you, my lord. Yes, I am.'

'William was just telling me about your visits to an area of poverty on the other side of the village.'

Her colour increased. 'Yes. The inhabitants don't have an easy life there. They are all extremely poor. The condition of the cottages is a disgrace, and they don't even have a covered drain. I am trying to persuade the men that it is better to have a covered drain than an open one, but it is an uphill fight. I don't suppose they've even thought about the advantages or disadvantages, and they have no idea about the health risks.'

Gareth's lips quivered. 'I imagine so. If you've never known any different, you don't understand why you should change anything. You see no point in the extra work. Especially so when a young lady comes along and tells you what to do.'

Julia's mother said, 'I keep telling her it is hazardous for her to go there, my lord. Heaven knows what she could pick up. But she won't listen.'

'Who owns the cottages?'

'I don't know,' Julia replied. 'Someone comes to collect the rent, but he's never been there when I've visited, and the people themselves don't ask such things. They are not on good terms with the rent collector, as you can imagine.'

The marquess viewed her thoughtfully for a moment before he nodded, and the conversation moved on to the delights of the present weather. Lady Stratton delayed for a moment to talk to Maria Dutton about the forthcoming invitation. The marquess and his friend were already out of sight by the time Julia and her mother wandered back through the village to their home and their Sunday occupations. They were both pleased to receive such an invitation, each for their own reasons. These days, invitations were few and far between. Lady Stratton looked forward to it because it would remind her of happier days when life was much richer, and Julia looked forward to seeing Hugh Grenville again. She was also curious about Cobham Abbey and its owner. He seemed haughty and arrogant in comparison with Hugh Grenville; but she was honest enough to admit their circumstances were completely different, and social position governed how someone was expected to conduct himself, and how he appeared to others.

4

'Would the ladies like the hood up, sir?'

The vicar looked enquiringly at them. Julia's pleading expression decided it. 'Leave it down!' he answered with a laugh. 'The weather is good today, and it is a short journey.'

'Very well, sir. I was told to drive you straight to the bottom of the hill overlooking the abbey. That's where you are expected.' The driver climbed onto his box seat, flicked his whip, and they set off.

They all enjoyed the novelty of driving in such a fashionable vehicle, and the short journey was soon over. Once they descended from the carriage at the foot of the hill, the driver turned the pair of matching horses and set off towards the stables on the far side of Cobham Abbey. They could see that the others were already making themselves comfortable up above on the gentle hill. Hugh Grenville spotted them and came down part of the way to meet them. It was an easy climb.

Julia noticed the marquess talking to a pretty woman in a pale cream muslin dress. She looked engrossed in their conversation and played with her parasol. His white shirt and neck-cloth, ruffled by the breeze, peeped out from beneath a pale grey waistcoat with metal buttons. His usual forbidding expression was more relaxed and hassle-free this afternoon.

When Hugh led them to him, his expression settled into a more sober expression. He dipped his chin; his voice was welcoming but coloured in neutral shades. 'I'm glad you could come. Please make yourselves comfortable and enjoy the day. You already know everyone, William, but Lady Stratton and Miss Julia don't. If you'll come with me, I'll introduce you to the others and then you will be free to go where you like and do as you wish.'

He signalled his departure to the young woman at his side briefly. Julia noticed she had golden ringlets and bright blue eyes, and her dress was decorated with frills and embroidered with pink flowers. It suited her. She looked like a porcelain shepherdess.

The marquess turned away and they followed. He stopped in front of a tall, elegant woman with dark hair that was going grey at the temples. She was standing at a distance from the others and looking thoughtfully down towards Cobham Abbey. There was something about her that reminded Julia of the marquess. She had a serious, reserved air.

He introduced them. 'Mother, you already know William and Mrs Dutton.'

'Good afternoon, Mrs Dutton, Dr Dutton! I'm pleased to see you again.'

'This is Lady Stratton and her daughter Miss Julia Stratton. They helped me when my phaeton went off the road the other day.'

Lady de Vere eyed them for a

moment and managed the beginning of a smile. 'I thank you for the help you gave my son. I think my husband knew your husband, didn't he, Mrs Stratton? I seem to remember his name. They met several times at Royal Society meetings.'

Lady Stratton curtseyed briefly. 'Yes, they did meet a couple of times, your ladyship. They seem to have had similar interests. We were only too pleased to help his lordship. Thankfully he has fully recovered.'

'Yes, so it seems. Please make yourself comfortable. I prefer to remain in the shade of the trees, but if one of you is a sun worshiper, we have chosen the right day. I was just thinking, Gareth, that this is a lovely spot. Much nicer than the other side of the hill.' She turned away, saying, 'I hope to talk with you all later.'

Julia's mother nodded and they followed the marquess, who was already moving towards the rest of the party. They exchanged words of introduction with his sister and her husband, a squire and his wife from the neighbouring estate, Cobham's present cleric who was already busy eyeing the food, and another couple who were on a short visit to Cobham Abbey. Lastly he led them back to the young woman with the parasol. 'This is Miss Charlotte Dandridge. She is a close friend of my sister, and a friend of the family.'

Charlotte Dandridge viewed them and they all bobbed politely. She noted they weren't dressed in the very height of fashion, but their apparel wasn't old-fashioned. It was of excellent quality, and well-made. She wondered briefly how ordinary people living in a country village could afford to dress so well.

Julia was almost glad when the marquess excused himself by saying he had promised to help his nephew fly his kite. He left them to their own devices. Miss Dandridge mentioned the weather again briefly, and remembered something she had to tell the marquess's sister straight away.

Julia's mother and Mrs Dutton decided to sit near the picnic spread out on the ground and sat down awkwardly on a plaid blanket. Dr Dutton began a desultory conversation with his fellow clergyman. It looked like most people intended to remain where they were. Thomas the butler was in charge of liquid refreshment, and there were other servants busy serving dishes and replacing used plates.

Julia was too restless to envisage sitting all afternoon. When her mother and Mrs Dutton started chatting about village affairs, she moved away. Mrs Dutton was glad of Lady Stratton's company. Did she feel uncomfortable in such illustrious circles? Julia's family was not noble, but her father was a gentleman and her mother was a baron's youngest daughter. Julia knew how to act among society, even though they were now no longer part of the *ton*. Her mother had been determined that she be well brought up, though her father had enjoyed seeing her competing with her brother and being more unladylike.

She viewed the food on the tablecloth. Its edges ruffled in the breeze. There was chicken pudding, a joint of cold beef, pigeon and onion pies, and cold tongue as well as tarts, cold desserts, various cheeses, bowls of fresh strawberries, several kinds of other fruit, fresh drinks and strawberry punch. Julia compared the feast of food with what the people in the ramshackle houses ate. She reminded herself to accept reality and just enjoy the day. Invitations like this wouldn't come her way very often anymore.

She moved away and leaned against a nearby tree. There was a deep blue sky above, and a chatter of birdsong from nearby greenery. She gazed down at Cobham Abbey. The spot had been well chosen. An avenue of trees led up to the main building from the distant entrance to the park, and there were long wings extending right and left of the lengthy frontage with rows of long windows, and dormer windows in the attics. The front entrance had a portico that sported classical columns. A dome-shaped roof in the middle of the main section heightened her belief that there was probably an impressive entrance hall. From where she stood, she had an excellent view of the extensive gardens and she could pick out the shape of formal beds, a walled kitchen garden, and a tasteful Italian Garden. Shrubberies here and there had not been neglected, and Julia imagined that there was much pleasure to be had from taking walks in the garden and the surrounding parkland. She also knew from Mrs Dutton that the house was listed in the *Traveller's Guide Book* and that its owner allowed visitors to view it on certain days. The blue dining room and the entrance hall received special mentions. Perhaps she'd make the effort to visit it one day, when the family was not at home. It looked like a delightful place.

Hugh Grenville interrupted her contemplations. 'Miss Stratton, I've taken the liberty of bringing you something to drink.'

She took the glass and sipped at the fresh lemonade. 'That was kind of you, Mr Grenville. I was just admiring the view.'

'Yes, it's a very good view of Cobham and the park. And we're extremely lucky with the weather today.'

Everywhere golden afternoon light blanketed the surroundings, the aroma of sunned grass filled the air, and warm breezes teased wisps from her carefully arranged hairstyle. She agreed heartily. 'It's perfect.' She looked down again. 'Was Cobham Abbey really an abbey? It doesn't have the right shape.'

He followed her glance. 'It was, a long time ago, but Henry VIII dissolved it and pocketed its treasures. Elizabeth I gave it to Gareth's family as a gift. They demolished the ruins later and this house was built last century.'

'You and the marquess are good friends?'

'Yes, we've known each other for almost twenty years.'

She smiled at him. 'It's good to have

friends, isn't it? My best friend lives where we came from and we keep in touch by letters. We don't see each other often enough. I'm looking forward to seeing her again soon. My aunt has invited me to stay with them in London for a couple of weeks. My uncle is a successful lawyer and my aunt sends me regular invitations. She thinks I must feel wretched because we now live in a country village with little social life.'

'And do you — feel wretched?'

She cradled her glass. 'No; strangely enough, I don't. I like the quiet rhythm of country life, and there are some really nice people living in the village. I've always loved reading, and there is a good lending library in the next town. My mother also now accepts that I actually enjoy working in the garden!' He chuckled. 'Time doesn't hang heavy at all. Perhaps visiting London does help, but I have never been dissatisfied when it was time to return home.'

'Strange that we have not met there before now.'

'I was due to have my first season in the year my brother died, and the year after that my papa died, so I have never had the kind of season you've attended. My aunt started inviting me when I stopped wearing mourning, and I had a very enjoyable time even without the most famous assemblies or events.'

'When are you planning to visit?'

'In a month's time, for three or four weeks. The season won't be in full swing — it is still too early for that — but I don't mind. I'm looking forward to browsing the bookshops, a visit or two to the theatre, and seeing the latest attractions.'

'Really? I'll also be in London then. I have some business to settle with my family's solicitor. I think Gareth mentioned he has to visit London too, to confer about plans with his main agent and consult his bank manager. Perhaps we will meet?'

Julia didn't think that was likely but she smiled anyway. 'That would be a pleasure. My friend Amelia and her parents are staying for the whole season, but Amelia's mother wants to come early to do some advance shopping before the rush starts.'

He nodded. 'There are still events and assemblies going on all the time. A lot of people remain in London all year through, and need to be entertained.'

She tilted her head to the side and her eyes twinkled. 'You mean the ones who don't have a country estate or haven't been invited to visit someone else's for the summer? Do you have a town house?'

He smiled. 'Yes, but it is fairly humble, especially in comparison with Gareth's impressive one in Courtland Street.'

'I'm looking forward to my visit, even if it isn't at the height of the season. Amelia's parents always include me in their party and they know how grateful I am. It means my aunt and uncle don't feel they have to entertain me all the time.' She heard china plates rattling and looked around. 'Perhaps we should get something to eat before it's all gone.'

He laughed softly. 'That won't happen. I'm sure the servants have orders to keep the tablecloth laden with scrumptious temptations.'

'Have you eaten yet, Mr Grenville?'

'No, but it's a jolly good idea.' He eyed the women sitting on the ground near the tablecloth. 'It looks like some of the ladies haven't moved at all. Some of them are still sitting where they were when I arrived.'

Julia laughed. Hugh smiled, extended his arm, and Julia slipped hers through his. They made their way back to the others and chattered together like old friends.

Julia sat down for a moment to choose what to eat; and Caroline, the marquess's sister, started a conversation. 'It was good of you to help my brother the other day, Miss Stratton. He told us all about it.'

She liked the straightforward expression on her agreeable face. Julia doubted if he'd mentioned his gift of half a crown; she didn't intend to bring it up ever again either. 'I'm sure anyone in the same position would have done the same, your ladyship.'

'Please, my name is Caroline. I know that yours is Julia, and I hear that you are an avid gardener. I could stick to the rules of decorum and call you Miss Stratton all afternoon, and you me Lady Alden, but quite honestly that is such a bore! It is much easier to be courteous and friendly at the same time if you think someone is worth knowing.'

Julia coloured, and noted her hobby was known by one and all. 'I think my interest in gardening is unpopular with many, because they don't believe it is suitable work for a lady. But I enjoy it. I dislike needlework, I can't draw, I am only a passable singer, I have little opportunity to dance, and we don't have a piano so I can't play music. That leaves me with lots of time, and nothing apart from reading and writing letters to fill it with. Hence my affection for flowers and vegetables.'

Caroline laughed. 'I can see you are

as authentic and unusual as Hugh told me you were. I can sympathize about the needlework and the drawing. I dislike them too!' She looked around and her brow wrinkled. 'I wonder where my son is. He wanted to stay with the men in the stables but my husband insisted he toe the line for once and come with us this afternoon.'

'I think the marquess mentioned that he was going to help him fly a kite.'

'Oh, then they are on the other side of the hill. There is always more wind there, as I remember well from our childhood. Sometimes my brother surprises me completely. He gives our Ralph no special attention; indeed, he seems to ignore him most of the time, then he'll suddenly grab him, put him in front of him on his horse, and gallop off with him perched there to go riding for miles. Or like today, he'll suddenly do something to delight Ralph. Ralph adores him, and my husband is sometimes quite jealous of my brother.' She shook the crumbs from her dress and got to her feet awkwardly. 'I must find my husband and tell him. Perhaps we'll walk across to see them flying the kite. I wonder where he is?'

Julia looked around. 'He's over there, talking to Mr Grenville.'

'Oh yes. We must talk again, Julia. I wish I had more courage to ignore social customs and practices like you, but I don't need to rebel — my husband is very open-minded and generous, so I have no reason to break out of my golden cage.'

Julia helped herself to some strawberries and cream. She noticed that Lady de Vere had made herself comfortable against the trunk of a nearby oak tree. Her eyes were closed and she was immobile, so Julia thought she was asleep. She thought it would be an excellent idea to rest in the shade on the other side of the tree. Julia sat down as quietly as she could.

Lady de Vere opened her eyes and looked around. 'Oh, Miss Stratton!'

'I'm sorry, your ladyship. Did I

disturb you? I thought you were sleeping.' She made to get up again. 'I'll find somewhere else and leave you in peace.'

She brushed Julia's words aside and patted the ground. 'Sit down and tell me about yourself. I expect you miss your old home, and your old lifestyle?'

For a second or two, Julia was surprised that she knew about their circumstances, but then she would be automatically curious about people who'd aided her son. 'No, your ladyship, not anymore. It took me a little time to accept the inevitable after I realized we had to leave our home, but thankfully I'm endowed with an optimistic attitude that helps me accept reality. I only hope that my father didn't worry himself into his grave. He was already troubled because he knew that my brother's premature death would mean hardship and a different lifestyle for us when he died, as the estate was entailed. He wanted to make suitable arrangements, but his own unexpected death curtailed that as well.'

Julia recalled how doting her father had been and how much she missed him. She hastened to add, 'I am not complaining. We have a roof over our head and more than enough for our needs. I think it was harder for my mother when the time came to leave. She'd lost a son and then her husband within a short time, and they are buried in the local churchyard. She has been very brave about it all. Mostly for my sake, I'm sure. I think she has almost adjusted now.'

Lady de Vere looked determinedly ahead, but she nodded and said brusquely, 'When you marry, things will change for the better.'

Julia laughed and replied, 'I don't expect to marry — not ever, your ladyship. I have no dowry, and living as we do in the country I am not likely to meet many men who are looking for someone like me. Prospective husbands expect a settlement; I don't have one.' She smiled and laughed softly. 'I don't mind. It doesn't worry me; in fact it makes me feel freer. I am my own master. I'm not unhappy with my prospects. My mother and I lead comfortable lives in comparison to many others. I haven't a wish to marry anyone, although I will miss not having any children.'

Lady de Vere looked suitably shocked. 'It would be wicked if a pretty girl like you wasted her life. What happens when you are alone in the world? Do you have any relatives?'

'Yes, but I won't be a burden. I hope that Mama and I will share many happy years together. We have talked about it and she understands how I feel. The cottage belongs to Mama and she will leave it to me with her settlement money. That is all we have at present too, and we manage very well. I hope to find some way of supplementing our income a little, now we are settled.'

Lady de Vere viewed the young woman with her forthright expression and determined words. 'I like strong women, Miss Stratton. And I think you are very strong.'

* * *

Later that afternoon, the marquess wondered if he should remind Hugh once again that Miss Stratton was not the catch of the season, even if she was pretty, intelligent and had a pleasant character. He had been watching them together a few minutes ago and couldn't remember when Hugh had last paid so much attention to a fleeting acquaintance. Perhaps it was because of the limited society at Cobham. He noticed that Hugh wasn't enamoured of Charlotte Dandridge; in fact, he seemed to avoid her. He understood that. Charlotte came from a good family and was fine in a certain way, but she was rather insipid. She was also a mite too pleasing whenever they conversed. He'd already crossed her off his list of 'possibilities'.

He knew Hugh well enough to tell whether he liked a woman or not. Miss Stratton had touched a soft spot in the man's heart. Perhaps it was just as well that they were all leaving Cobham soon for London. Hugh would find plenty of other diversions there, and they'd meet lots of old friends. Miss Stratton would fade quickly from everyone's memory when there were other distractions.

5

It was too early in the season to be caught up in masses of excitement, but Julia didn't mind. In comparison to her quiet life at home, there was always something new to see, somewhere to go in London. Her aunt and uncle were kind and very understanding. Their own daughter was married and living in Devon. Julia's aunt enjoyed her niece's visits and did all she could to make her stay a pleasant one. She loved Julia for the courageous way she'd come to terms with her new situation.

If her aunt was unable to accompany Julia on her excursions for some reason, she sent her maid as a replacement. Julia tried to persuade her aunt that it didn't matter much anymore if she was unaccompanied, because she was no longer in the marriage market, but the older woman still insisted that London was no place for a young unmarried woman to wander around on her own. Julia loved her excursions to the park, along the better-known streets, to the shops, and to the libraries and book-shops where she was free to peruse at leisure what was on offer. She tried to store it all in her memory for the quieter days when she was home again. She'd arrived by stagecoach a couple of days ago. A neighbour had kindly offered to accompany her, as he had business in London.

She was now looking forward to Amelia's arrival. They'd have a couple of weeks together to talk about fashion, about London, and Amelia's future. It was clear that Amelia's parents hoped that she would meet a prospective husband this season. Amelia was two years younger than Julia. Her parents were landed gentry, so if she attracted attention, it was likely to be from a younger son or someone whose riches came from newer sources, rather than an aristocratic background. Amelia's family was not likely to get vouchers for Almack's. Only the highest social rank of gentlemen seeking brides of suitable *ton*, or young ladies with the highest aristocratic connections seeking suitable husbands, were accepted there. However, Julia was sure her friend would still enjoy the assemblies and events planned to make her season an enjoyable one.

Sitting with her aunt one morning, Julia was chatting about her friendship with Amelia. Her aunt reached across and patted her knee. 'You know how much I regret that you won't have the same chances as your friend Amelia, don't you? It is a dreadful shame that John hadn't arranged a marriage for you before he died.'

Julia smiled at her. 'I don't think Papa even wanted an arranged marriage for me, Aunt. He wanted me to be happy! If I had been a boy, everything would have been fine, whereas — '

'Whereas you and your mama have been left adrift!'

Julia shrugged. 'Mama and I manage

very well. You invite me to visit you from time to time so I am not quite the rustic yet — especially with regard to fashions. It is one of Mama's greatest pleasures when you send the latest Ackermann's illustrations. She busies herself with altering our dresses to be à la mode. Not that many people in the village notices when she does, but it keeps her occupied and her mind on other things.'

'Your mama always was an accomplished needlewoman.' She viewed her niece's dress. 'And no one would suspect that you live permanently in the country, because she keeps you right up to the mark.'

Julia laughed softly. 'Yes, she does, bless her! I wish I could persuade her to visit London instead of me. She insists our finances don't stretch to two of us visiting London at the same time, and she thinks it's more important for me to be here than to come herself. I suspect she still hopes I'll chance across some unsuspecting rich man.'

Her aunt shook her head and laughed. 'There are lots of decent men who would be proud to call you their wife. Perhaps not from the kind of circles you could have expected a couple of years ago, but there are a lot of respectable professions with eligible bachelors on the lookout.'

'If I was interested that would be fine, but I'm not, and I am happy to be single.'

'Ah! But what about the time when you are old and alone?'

'I've thought about that. I think I'll always enjoy books and my garden, and I know a lot of people in the village already so I won't be alone. We manage financially and I think that will continue. I won't miss the success of the marriage market.' Julia wanted to change the subject. 'I'd intended to look for some dress material for Mama this morning. She said she thought you'd help me choose because you have such good taste. She gave me all the measurements and her suggestions for which materials she thought might be suitable.'

Her aunt put down her cup of cocoa. 'Then that's what we'll do.'

They took her aunt's coach to Pall Mall. Her coachman doubled up as her aunt's footman, so they felt quite safe. They spent an enjoyable morning, and the man behind the counter helped them choose a length of dark blue cotton batiste and matching narrow braid.

Her aunt looked around and commented, 'It's clear to see the season is not in full swing yet.

'Very true, madam. In a couple of weeks you might have to queue and wait for someone to serve you.'

With their purchase in brown paper and string, they returned for a light luncheon. Julia then declared she wanted to go to a bookshop on the other side of a nearby park. Her aunt waved the idea aside. 'I'm going to lie down for an hour. Take Maggie with you! And wear boots. It rained in the night, and if you go to the park, the ground will probably be muddy.'

Julia set off with Maggie in tow. She had the feeling the young servant was happy in her role of a chaperone, as it took her away from her duties to places she'd never usually go, though she complained continually about her feet. The weather was good. The sky was blue and white clouds hopped across the sky, driven by light winds. They walked through the park and along the adjoining street, where Julia was automatically drawn to Hatchards with its bow windows displaying the newest books on offer.

She fingered the half crown Marquess de Vere had given her in her reticule, then smiled to herself and gazed at the books on offer. Maggie declared she couldn't understand for her life why books were so interesting, but then Maggie couldn't read. Julia deliberated if she should go inside and take a closer look at the multitude of other books on offer. She wanted to prolong the pleasure of choosing a book before she left.

Lots of people were parading along

the pavement, and coaches and riders were busy on the road. Her hair was piled high on her head with wisps about her face. She tightened the ribbons on her poke bonnet and straightened her spencer. Maggie was full of curiosity and eyed the people in passing. She commented on their clothes and their appearance. Julia only needed to agree or disagree with her comments. Suddenly she did notice two men she knew, with a lady riding between their mounts, coming towards them. As they drew abreast and came to a standstill, Julia coloured a little.

Hugh Grenville tipped his hat and gave her a warm smile of recognition. His horse pranced nervously. 'Miss Stratton! How nice to see you!'

She looked up at him and returned his smile. 'Likewise, Mr Grenville.' She bobbed in the direction of the others. 'Your lordship.'

De Vere acknowledged by touching the brim of his top hat. 'Good morning, Miss Stratton.' He indicated the beauty between them. 'May I introduce Lady Harriet Pargetter.'

The blond beauty in her jaunty riding dress and saucy green hat, with its small feather fluttering in the breeze, eyed Julia from her elevated position and checked her companion's expression before she finally tipped her chin. Julia responded accordingly.

Hugh asked, 'How long have you been in London? And what are you doing here?'

She smiled at Hugh. 'Just over a week, and at present I was just about to go into the shop to find an interesting book.'

'Well you've chosen the right bookshop. They have an amazing variety.'

'Yes, I know. I was here very often with my father. He was an avid reader and we often came out with several bands under our arms. They were often about obscure subjects. Papa always insisted unusual subjects made more interesting reading, and I must admit most of the time he was right.'

The marquess felt obliged to say something. 'Are you enjoying London?'

'Yes. I'm staying with my aunt and uncle and they are doing their best to make my visit very enjoyable. A dear friend of mine is arriving in a day or two, and her parents will include me in their excursions, so I am looking forward to that too.'

Hugh asked, 'Will you be attending any of the assemblies? The season is gradually warming up.'

She nodded. 'I think we will, although I don't know their definite plans yet.'

'Where does your aunt live?'

'Great Russell Street.'

'That's not far from the British Museum.'

'I know. My aunt tries to stop me going there so often, but there is so much to see. It's quite fascinating.'

'I live near here in Albany Street.'

Julia nodded and noticed that the marquess didn't offer any information as to where his town house was. His brows were drawn in a straight line.

Lady Pargetter was looking around to see if there were any of her acquaintances in sight.

Hugh ploughed on. 'I'll call one day, if I may. Perhaps we can share a drive around the park one afternoon?'

Julia's expression mirrored her appreciation. 'That would be fun.'

'Good! Then we'll meet again soon. I hope you find a good book.'

'So do I!' She bobbed briefly. 'Good afternoon, Mr Grenville, your lordship, my lady. It was a pleasure to meet you.'

'The pleasure was all ours, Miss Stratton,' said Hugh.

The marquess touched the brim of his hat. 'Good afternoon!'

Miss Pargetter was already fiddling with the reins, anxious to steer her horse back among all the other traffic going in the right direction. They were all accomplished riders and elegantly dressed. Maggie had remained silent and frozen to the spot.

'Cor! Wot a couple of swells! She was snooty, but the gents were regular out-and-outers!'

Julia laughed softly as she listened to Maggie's Cockney comments. 'Yes, I agree, they are.' She turned to the entrance door. She didn't really expect to see Hugh again, but it was kind of him to stop and exchange a few words. She spent some time choosing her book and finally settled on a travel digest about Italy. She would pack it in her suitcase and thoroughly enjoy reading about a place she'd never seen in real life when she returned home. She'd paid for her book from her spending money and hadn't used her half crown. It was still safely stored away in her reticule.

Outside again, she hurried Maggie along. The servant complained that her shoes were hurting, but Julia paid little attention. She'd discovered that Maggie always complained if she had to walk further than the end of the street. They had to be home in time to change for the evening meal. Her aunt and uncle followed style and custom as much as their finances allowed, and changing every evening for the meal was one of those customs. Julia didn't mind, as it gave her a chance to wear some of her mother's new or altered creations. Her uncle had bought tickets for the theatre that evening, and she was looking forward to it very much.

* * *

Later, with Maggie's clever fingers coaxing a fashionable hairstyle, and in her gown with its gauze overdress, Julia felt attractive and pretty.

She received several admiring glances when they entered and made their way to their places in the theatre. Some were of genuine admiration, while others were sensory and made her feel uncomfortable. The play was well performed, and Julia was entranced and fully engrossed by the happenings on stage.

In one of the boxes, she was unaware that Marquess de Vere was sitting with a group of friends and acquaintances. One of the men was scouring the audience with his glass. His view lingered on Julia. 'Lord! A new face; and a fine filly she is, too.'

The others followed the direction of his interest. There was a general murmur of assent and comments. Someone said, 'Yes, a tempting armful! Who is she?' No one knew. Their attention wandered elsewhere.

Gareth didn't mention that he knew her. For some reason he was irritated that the others viewed her like a prize filly. He remained in the shadows and busy with his own thoughts. Harriet Pargetter had the right background, and she could hold a fairly intelligent conversation, but somehow the idea of seeing her across the dining table for the rest of his life was not appealing.

* * *

The next morning Amelia arrived. She came to see Julia straight away, just before luncheon. Her blond curls peeped out from her bonnet, her blue eyes sparkled, and her face was excited.

After embracing, and still slightly out of breath, she said, 'We arrived quite early this morning. We stopped on the outskirts of London overnight and started out at the crack of dawn. Isn't London exhilarating? So much hustle and bustle, so much noise, so many coaches and riders — it takes your breath away. I couldn't wait to see you. Mama and Papa want to invite you, and your aunt and uncle, to high tea this afternoon. They are looking forward to seeing you, Julia, and Mama wants to talk to your aunt about what is planned and get her permission to include you in our arrangements.'

Julia smiled at her friend. 'It is so good to see you. I would love to come.' She turned to her aunt. 'And you, Aunt?'

Her aunt nodded, watching the two girls indulgently. 'It will be a pleasure to meet your parents, Amelia. I am delighted that Julia will have the chance to visit events that I can no longer attend. Now that my own daughter is married and living elsewhere, I don't have the same motive to attend assemblies anymore. My husband usually disappears to the card room and then I find it all very boring.' Looking at her niece, she added, 'Of course Julia won't have the same motive, but she will enjoy herself I am sure.'

Quite innocently, Amelia answered, 'I suppose you mean finding a prospective husband? I think it's dreadful, but my parents are determined for me to attend and been seen. If Julia comes with us, it won't be so nerve-wracking, and it will give me more pleasure than you can imagine!' She stood up and jiggled the folds out of her dress. 'I can't stay — I promised to help Mama unpack and organize everything we brought with us — but I'm looking forward to seeing you later this afternoon.'

The butler entered with a small silver tray displaying a card. 'There is a Mr Hugh Grenville in the hall, madam. He asked if he might speak to Miss Julia.'

Julia coloured with pleasure. Her aunt's eyebrows lifted and Julia explained briefly how they had met and that he had promised to call. Her aunt nodded. 'Show the gentleman in, Thomas.'

With rounded eyes, Amelia sat down again and viewed Julia with a puzzled expression. Thomas returned with the caller at his heel. Hugh entered with the self-confidence of his upbringing. He handed his hat and gloves to the waiting butler. Thomas withdrew silently and Julia smiled at Hugh.

'Mr Grenville! How good of you to call so soon after our meeting. May I introduce you to my aunt, Mrs Downing, and my dear friend, Miss Amelia Wilcox?'

He bowed from the waist to her aunt, and then to Amelia, where his glance lingered longer. 'Ma'am! Miss Wilcox! It is a pleasure to meet you both. I was in the area this morning and decided on the spur of the moment to call on you, Miss Julia. I hope it's not inconvenient?'

'No, not at all.'

'I wanted to renew my promise to take you for a drive in my buggy — that is, of course, with your aunt's approval.' He gave her aunt a warm smile.

'May, I Aunt?'

She smiled. 'Of course, my dear. In an open carriage, in public, there is no reason you should not.'

Hugh's glance wandered to Amelia again, and after a pause he added, 'Perhaps I can persuade Miss Amelia to come with us? Then no one in the world could possibly object, could they?'

Amelia coloured. 'That is most kind of you, sir. I have just arrived in London and I long to take in as many sights as I can. I am sure my parents will not object if they know I am going with Julia.'

He nodded. 'If you are a newcomer, I expect you are looking forward to attending assemblies and such things?'

'Oh yes. I want to visit the zoo, go shopping, and drink a cup of chocolate at a café; go for walks with Julia, and attend theatres and concerts. Perhaps if I'm lucky I will even see the Prince

Regent.' Her enthusiasm was mirrored in her face and her blue eyes sparkled like sapphires.

Hugh thought she was extremely pretty and quite enchanting. Blonds were all the rage at the moment, and Hugh had no doubt that Miss Amelia Wilcox would cause a stir. 'The Regent isn't in town at present, as it is too early in the season for him yet, but I am sure you'll be able manage all the rest without any problem.' He dragged his attention back to Julia. She was pretty too, though completely different in colouring, and he decided the two of them together made a perfect contrast.

He waved away Julia's aunt's offer of refreshments. 'No, thank you, ma'am. I am meeting a friend and I must be on my way. When will our drive be convenient, Miss Julia?'

She replied, 'When does it suit you?'

Hugh liked the way she didn't pretend her daily plan was already full. Too many girls thought they heightened a man's interest by pretending they were in demand. 'What about the day after tomorrow? If Miss Wilcox has just arrived, she will need to unpack and do all the things that young ladies have to do first, before they can think of other things.'

Julia looked questioningly at Amelia, who nodded quickly. 'That will be fine, Mr Grenville. We will both look forward to seeing you.'

'I will bring my carriage here to fetch you.' He turned to Amelia. 'Would you like me to come for you too, Miss Wilcox?'

A little flustered, Amelia replied, 'No, please don't bother. I will come here and wait with Julia. What time?'

'Shall we say three o'clock? Then we will be able to drive in peace for a little while before most other people begin to think about driving through the parks.'

The two women smiled and nodded. Hugh took his leave and bowed to them all before he exited.

After a moment, Julia's aunt remarked, 'What a pleasant young man! How kind of him to call and offer to drive you around the park, Julia. You mentioned meeting him earlier in your letters, but I didn't think you'd hear from him ever again.'

Julia stared at the closed door. 'No, neither did I. I met him by chance yesterday. Hugh is a real gentleman, isn't he?'

* * *

Two days later, the two friends were ensconced in a town carriage drawn by a team of well-matched black horses. They entered Hyde Park with Hugh's groom up front, driving them at a sedate pace down Rotten Row. They had the excitement of seeing and being seen. Hugh was at his charming best. He endeavoured to point out any persons of standing whom they passed. The weather was perfect, and the two women soon understood why Hugh said that driving along Rotten Row was as much a social event as a form of exercise.

'The Prince of Wales drives here regularly when he's in London.' He didn't add that Prinny often drove around with his mistress at his side.

Hugh's information had the hoped-for effect. Amelia's eyes were round like saucers. 'Really?' She turned to her friend at her side. 'Isn't it exciting, Julia? And everyone is dressed so fashionably. I think Mama is right when she says we are dreadfully behind the times. I won't complain again when she insists we must visit the draper and dressmaker!'

Julia patted her friend's knee. 'People will always notice your face first and what you are wearing second. You do very well.'

Hugh smiled across at them. 'You are right, Julia. Miss Wilcox will stand out anywhere she goes.'

Amelia turned pink. 'Thank you, Mr Grenville. Would it be wrong to ask you to call me Amelia — if you call Julia by her name?'

Hugh looked pleased. 'I have known

Julia a little longer, but you are Julia's friend, and I don't think anyone could object — but only if in return you call me Hugh.'

Amelia's expression softened and her eyes looked warm and grateful. Julia smiled as she viewed her friend and Hugh. Her thoughts began to gallop along, and they were only interrupted when Marquess de Vere drew alongside on a large black steed. He held its impatient movements in check. He was dressed in stylish riding clothes and presented an impressive figure as he towered above them on his horse.

'Gareth! What are you doing here?'

The marquess tipped the rim of his hat with a gloved finger and nodded to the two women. 'The same as you, I expect. I'm exercising my horse and enjoying some fresh air.'

'You already know Julia, but may I introduce Miss Amelia Wilcox? She is visiting London for the season.'

Gareth nodded again in Amelia's direction. 'Your servant, Miss Wilcox.'

Hugh mentioned yesterday that he'd promised to take the two girls for a ride, and Gareth's curiosity was roused. Julia Stratton looked well, but he made no excuse to idle and engage her in conversation.

'I hope you enjoy the drive, ladies.' He turned to Hugh. 'I'll see you later at the club — or have you planned something else for this evening?'

'No; I've booked fencing exercises later, but nothing for this evening.'

'Good; I'll see you then, perhaps. Freddy Mortimer will be there. I met him a couple of minutes ago.' He reined in his impatient steed and tipped the brim of his hat again before he turned his horse in the opposite direction and galloped off at a faster pace.

Nothing could spoil the rest of the day for Amelia. She could call Mr Grenville by his first name, she had driven down Rotten Row, and she had been introduced to a real-life marquess.

6

The next couple of weeks were a round of pleasure for the two women. There were visits to the zoo and the Tower of London, walks along the approved parts of the city, evening entertainments at home, and a couple of invitations to other people's evening amusements. Julia had a pleasant voice and Amelia was an accomplished pianist, so they were often asked to perform. Julia didn't enjoy being in the limelight, but she was well liked for her modesty, and people soon understood that an invitation to Amelia had to include one for Julia as well.

The season was not yet in full swing, but assemblies took place throughout the year. Not all of London society had a country estate. People needed plenty of activities and attractions.

Mr Wilcox bought vouchers to attend

several assemblies soon after they arrived. At one of them they met Hugh again. He arrived late with a couple of other young men and looked pleased when he glanced around and spotted their party. He came over to address them, and he danced a country dance with both. Amelia's mother nodded her approval as she contentedly watched her daughter work her way down the line with him and figure their way up it again.

Julia was secretly disappointed not to see the marquess with him, but then reminded herself she couldn't expect to meet him again. They moved in different circles. Hugh and she chatted like old friends when it was her turn for him to guide her through the dance. She told him what they'd been doing and noticed how his glance drifted back to Amelia now and then. She was sitting demurely where they'd left her, by her mother's side.

Hugh explained, 'I only happened to call because Stephan's sister is here tonight and his mother insisted that he come and give her some attention. Stephan was at university with Gareth and me.' He smiled down at her. 'I'm now glad we came, but we are planning to leave as soon as tea is announced. There is a boxing spectacle we want to see a little later. Nevertheless, I hope to meet you and your friend again soon. I expect you noticed that a lot more people are beginning to return to town. The weather has been bad lately. Gareth went to see his agent in Devon, but he's since returned to London. His sister and mother have announced they are coming, and he wanted to check that the house was in order, and ready and waiting.'

The music was drawing to a close, and he offered his arm to escort her back to the others. He thanked her, bowed to both women, and stopped on his way back to his friends to talk to another man standing alongside the wall on the opposite side of the room. A short time later, he raised his hand in farewell as the group exited. They left behind several disappointed mamas and their daughters.

* * *

Amelia's mother had bright cheeks when Julia joined them the next morning after breakfast. 'My dear! What do you think has happened? I never expected such regard.'

Julia waited patiently and Amelia lifted her eyes to heaven.

'Lady Wilburton has invited us to her next soirée. It is all due to you.'

'Me?' Julia said. 'Please explain, Mrs Wilcox. I don't know Lady Wilburton. Who is she?'

She smiled. 'She is Mr Grenville's sister. They have a house in Wigmore Street. I presume that Mr Grenville has suggested our names and asked her to include us. Apparently it will be a small function — just fifty people, and some dancing.'

'Really? If that is the reason we received an invitation, it was kind of

Hugh, but I don't understand why he should single us out.'

Mrs Wilcox tapped her on her knee. 'Don't you? I think he has taken a shine to you, my dear.'

'I don't believe that, ma'am. Indeed I don't. He is pleasant and kind, but he knows I am no great catch. If he has brought us to the attention of his sister, then it is out of the kindness of his heart.'

'Well, no matter why. We must go to the dressmaker's straight away. Amelia has nothing suitable; she must have a white dress with a gauze overdress with rosebuds worked around the neckline and on the hem. Maggie can weave fresh pink rosebuds into her hair. That would be perfectly suitable, and she will look beautiful.'

Julia smiled at her friend. 'I'm sure she will.'

'And what about you? Has your mama made something suitable? If not, we will order something at the same time for you.'

Julia shook her head and her curls swayed around her face. 'There is no need for that, ma'am. Are you sure I am included in the invitation?'

'Yes, quite clearly.'

'How kind! I have a pale lemon dress that will suit very well. It has a ruffled embroidered hem, short sleeves and a square neckline bordered with lace. I only brought it because Mama insisted I needed something in case we attended some special event.'

Amelia's mother nodded. 'Good. I'll just give the cook instructions about the meal this evening and then we can be off to the draper's. The dressmaker will have to be quick.' She got up and bustled out of the door.

After she'd left, Amelia was quiet for a moment before she asked what she was longing to know. 'You don't think Mr Grenville has taken a shine to you, Julia?'

'No, I don't. He is a delightful man to talk with and I do like him, but that is all. If he has a hand in this invitation, then it is extremely kind of him to remember some people that he hardly knows.'

Amelia looked happier. 'Yes, it is. Mama warned me before we came that we could not expect many invitations from upper society. But I must admit, I am looking forward to seeing Mr Grenville again.'

Julia guessed why, but busied herself with studying the carpet and didn't comment.

* * *

The following Friday, Mr Wilcox's coach drew up outside the given address. They had to wait in line for other coaches to deposit their passengers, and for servants with torches to light their way up the entrance steps. The four of them were in various stages of apprehension as they went inside and removed their cloaks. They joined a line of people waiting to shake hands with their host and hostess.

Lord and Lady Wilburton were standing at the door leading to a long room with gilded mirrors on all the walls, and where delicate-looking chairs were placed at suitable spots for visitors to sit. There was the sweet smell of gardenia in the air, coming from large pots of flowers in a couple of recesses.

Mr Wilcox gave a short bow and said, 'Your ladyship, your lordship, may I introduce my wife Mrs Wilcox, my daughter Amelia and her friend Miss Stratton.'

The Wilburtons smiled politely, shook their hands, and invited them to find a comfortable spot and help themselves to food from the buffet and drinks from the servants in the adjoining room.

Mr Wilcox led his party across the room and they took their place in a niche. Mr and Mrs Wilcox sat down and the two young women sat between them. Mr Wilcox soon left them to obtain some drinks and came back with lemonade for everyone. The room was already crowded, but people were still arriving, and Mrs Wilcox declared it would be a delightful crush. A small orchestra was playing softly in the background, and Julia was sure that when their hosts knew the majority of people had arrived, they would then instruct the musicians to supply dance music.

Mr Wilcox spied someone that he knew, and the two men met midway and wandered off into the adjoining room together.

Mrs Wilcox sniffed annoyingly. 'I hope your papa has not deserted us for the rest of the evening, Amelia.'

Amelia looked like an angel in her white dress with its pink roses. 'Mama, you know very well that Papa will not abandon us for long. Let him enjoy himself a little. He dislikes dancing, so he will only be bored.'

Mrs Wilcox employed her fan and uttered, 'You are right, my dear. Your papa is a good man and his main concern is always his family. We come first with him always.'

Amelia looked up and turned pink.

'Oh look! Mr Grenville is coming our way.'

With a broad smile, Hugh bowed. 'Mrs Wilcox, Amelia, Julia! I am glad to see you here this evening.'

Mrs Wilcox rattled on, 'I have a feeling we should thank you that your sister invited us, Mr Grenville. I have not met her previously, although I have seen her at some gatherings and knew who she was, of course.'

Hugh didn't disagree or concur. He looked at the two young women, perhaps for a moment or two longer when his eyes rested on Amelia. 'I came to ask if these ladies will include me on their dance cards before all the young men descend to beg the same of the prettiest ones in the room.'

Julia looked up and smiled. 'There are many pretty ladies, but I thank you for the compliment and I will be delighted.'

His eyes twinkled. 'Good.'

Julia continued, 'What about one of the country dances? There are a few spread throughout the evening entertainment.'

He nodded and watched her pencil in one of the dances halfway through the evening. He then turned his attention to Amelia. 'And will you give me the honour of the first dance, Amelia?'

Amelia was a little flustered. She said haltingly, 'The first of the evening?'

'Yes!'

Amelia looked down and busied herself with her card. 'Oh, thank you! There, I have entered your name.'

Hugh looked pleased and bowed briefly before he moved away again.

Mrs Wilcox looked delighted. 'Good heavens, what an honour! Fancy him asking you to dance the first of the evening, Amelia. He must know many other young ladies who are hoping to catch his attention. Such a good-looking man, with such fine manners! I declare I have never met anyone nicer.' Spreading her fan, she began to cool her face and looked towards the adjoining room, hoping to see the return of her husband. She longed to tell him how Hugh Grenville had singled their daughter out. It was going to be the best evening she'd experienced in London since they'd arrived.

To the surprise of the two young women, several other men hurried to be included in their dance cards, and they were soon almost full. Julia watched happily as her friend took the floor with Hugh for the first dance. They were an attractive couple. Amelia looked like a porcelain shepherdess, and Hugh danced well and was an elegant figure in a dark green topcoat and gold waistcoat.

Whenever she was engaged to dance, Julia could afford to feel relaxed and enjoy herself. There was no necessity to make conversation with men she would never meet again. Some of them chatted with her as they danced, while others were more aloof and seemed to be concentrating on merely looking noble and effective at her side.

The room grew warmer as the evening progressed, and Mr Wilcox returned only to busy himself with procuring his party with something to drink again. After a while, a gentleman approached and bowed from the waist briefly. 'Good evening! My name is Fenton Dantes. I am a cousin of the Marquess de Vere. I believe you know him?'

Mr Wilcox tipped his chin. 'We have not had the pleasure, sir, but Julia knows him, and we have all met his friend Mr Hugh Grenville.'

'I have heard the name Julia Stratton mentioned a couple of times.' His eyes raked the two women. He was tall and slim, too slim, with a pale complexion. He wore a black and silver tailcoat and a striped black and white waistcoat. His jet-black hair was drawn into a loose bunch at the nape of his neck and held in place there by a black ribbon. His face was thin with hollow cheeks, his eyes dark and lustrous. A quizzing glass hung from his waistcoat, and a large square-cut emerald twinkled in the candlelight whenever he moved his long fingers. He leaned forward slightly and smiled. 'I hope there are still some dances free?'

If he was related to the marquess, Mr and Mrs Wilcox presumed that he must be a proper gentleman. Julia wondered briefly why he'd sought them out. Hugh's sister must have invited him, but if he was a relation of the de Vere family that was not surprising. The two families were probably closely acquainted.

Mr and Mrs Wilcox were too overwhelmed to reply, so Julia said, 'With pleasure, Mr Dantes.' She showed him her card and he pointed. Julia filled his name against the chosen one. More hesitatingly, Amelia did the same. He bowed again and moved off. Julia watched him as he joined a small group of men standing together on the side. They were all too ostentatiously dressed. He lowered his head to talk to one of them, who was his direct neighbour. He looked deliberately in their direction, and the man followed his glance and laughed. Somehow Julia doubted that they were men of delicate scruples, but on the other hand he was the marquess's cousin.

'Well I never!' Mrs Wilcox said. 'Just imagine that. To have the attention of the cousin of the Marquess de Vere! I think our stay in London is going to be a resounding success, Amelia.'

Juliet smiled and tried to ignore the uncertainty Fenton Dantes had aroused in her. If Amelia felt misgivings about him, she neither mentioned it nor showed it in any way. She merely nodded at her mother's remark and studied her dancing card.

* * *

The evening was a success, because the two young women did not lack for partners; partially because the young men were impressed by Amelia's looks and grace, and partially because the first dance with Hugh had established her position and made her and her party acceptable to all present. If anyone knew of Julia's lower status, they did not show it.

Mr and Mrs Wilcox looked on with satisfaction when, after the first dance, Hugh escorted Amelia across the room and presented her to his sister and his brother-in-law. They exchanged a few sentences, and then Hugh brought her back and asked for a second dance later in the evening before he left.

A couple of dances later, Fenton Dantes came to lead Amelia onto the floor. Julia had no partner for the dance, so she could watch them. He was an elegant figure, but there was also an air of arrogance about him. Julia compared him to the marquess; but whereas the marquess had reasons to be arrogant, Fenton Dantes didn't. He spoke to his partner rarely, and his expression was pretentious. He didn't resemble his cousin closely. They were both dark, but Dantes had edges to his profile that were too sharp and he had an unhealthy colour. They were both tall and slim, but the marquess's hair was dark brown, his complexion was fresh, and his clothes were elegantly restrained and of the best quality. He wore the family signet ring on his little finger and a watch fob, nothing else in the way of jewellery.

Two dances later, it was Julia's turn to dance with Fenton Dantes, and he was more talkative with her than he had been with Amelia. 'I hear that you know Gareth?'

Julia was an accomplished dancer, so she could afford to answer without losing her step. 'The word 'know' is a slight exaggeration, sir. I have met him once or twice. And I attended a picnic at Cobham Abbey recently. I live nearby.'

'Ah! Cobham. A delightful place! Do you know that I'm Gareth's heir, until he has a legitimate son?'

Julia thought it was an odd remark to make to a stranger. 'No, I didn't. I have no knowledge of the family. It was pure chance that I met him at all.'

'And what do you think of him?'

Julia didn't like the way he was probing and fishing, obviously for negative responses. 'He's polite and well liked by his local tenants. My mother and I are familiar with Dr Dutton, the local cleric. He knows the marquess very well and also what local people think about their landlord. Apparently he's very fair and just.'

Fenton Dantes grimaced. 'Ah yes! Dutton, he used to be Gareth's tutor.' They parted in the dance for a moment. When they rejoined he said, 'Dutton is a dull dog, and he's not likely to say anything discreditable about Gareth, is he? He knows which side of his bread is buttered.'

Her anger awakened, Julia replied, 'Vicar Dutton is a highly intelligent man, and he is very respected and liked in the community. He doesn't lie, and he has no reason to ingratiate himself. Indeed, the marquess is the one who seeks Dr Dutton out, not the other way round.'

He viewed her speculatively. 'Gareth has made an impression on you, hasn't he?'

Julia coloured a little. 'Not in the way

you are inferring, sir. You asked what I thought of him, and I told you.'

'And my aunt? What a formidable woman she is. Don't you agree?'

'I don't know Lady de Vere either. I have only met her once, very briefly. Her social status demands her to be strong-minded. Being resolute does not automatically mean that she is cold or unfeeling.'

'My aunt is one of the most undemonstrative, taciturn people I have ever met.'

Julia shrugged. 'I have no idea how many people are dependent on the marquess for their living, but it must be a considerable number. Your aunt was at the heart of running the various estates with her husband for many years. It has formed her. I was always surprised how unemotional my own father was when he settled controversial estate affairs. He was never unfeeling, but I'm sure our workers sometimes thought he was harsh or hard-hearted. He took decisions that were to everyone's benefit, even if some tenants didn't appreciate it at the time.'

He looked surprised. 'Your father has an estate?'

'No. My father died recently, and the estate was entailed.'

His eyes were chilled. 'Oh! What bad luck, my dear! Still, I'm sure that someone with your looks will have no trouble finding someone to look after you. You can always try to charm Gareth.'

All her previous nervousness returned, and Julia looked forward to the end of the dance. When it ended, he offered his arm and she had no alternative. He led her back to the Wilcox party. As they drew closer, Julia was surprised to see the marquess standing nearby with two other men and two young ladies. He was watching them.

Fenton Dantes saw him too, and his expression changed briefly. He couldn't conceal his animosity. He dipped his head and guided Julia towards his cousin.

'Ah, Gareth! I didn't expect to see you here. Isn't this evening a bit below you? There are actually people present who don't have a title.' He gave him a cloying smile and played with his quizzing glass.

'Like yourself! I'm surprised to see you here, Dantes. Are the gambling tables shut down this evening? Where is your retinue of ninny-hammers? Or are they still ape-drunk from yesterday's outing?' The marquess's brows were drawn in a straight line, his voice restrained but laced with disdain. He wanted to annoy, and succeeded. Fenton's expression darkened.

Julia stood silently. The two men were related, but there was no love lost between them. After a moment de Vere suddenly remembered she was present when Fenton patted her hand. She had to stop herself withdrawing her arm.

'I believe you already know Miss Stratton. I am about to restore her to her party.'

'There is no need, Fenton. Miss Stratton has obliged me with the next dance.' He offered his arm. Julia took it quickly. Fenton looked at them both, bowed momentarily, and then disappeared into the nearby crush of people. He led her towards the dance floor.

'There is no need for you to dance with me, my lord. I can tell you wanted to evade your cousin. Please don't disappoint your friends. It will suffice if you take me back to my party.'

He looked solemn, but somewhere at the back of his dark eyes there was amusement. 'Then I would lose the opportunity of dancing with you, Miss Stratton.'

'With all respect, my lord, you know very well that society will only gossip if you waste your time on someone like me.'

'Someone like you? What do you mean?'

'Someone beneath your standing.'

He stopped for a moment and she was forced to turn a little and face him. 'I may be many things, Miss Stratton, but I am not a snob who looks down on others. You also just helped me to end an unwelcome encounter with Fenton.

I've met your mother and you've met some of my family. I think it makes dancing with each other for a couple of minutes highly appropriate, don't you?'

He guided her towards the dance floor and Julia no longer resisted. As they went, he declared, 'As you noticed, my cousin and I are not the best of friends. I won't bore you with why; just accept that it is the case.'

She nodded and prepared to take her place in the country dance. 'I think there is generally someone in one's family that you can't abide, isn't there? I have a great aunt called Agatha who puts the fear of God into me. She has done so since I was small. Whenever I visit her, she spends all the time preaching about hell and damnation and telling me that is where I am surely going to end up if I don't improve my manners and behaviour. Thank heaven I don't need to see her often because she lives near the Scottish border, and especially now because our means don't run to casual visits anymore.'

The corners of his mouth turned up. 'She sounds like a formidable woman.'

'She's horrifying. I keep telling myself I'm a grown-up, independent woman, but when I think about Aunt Agatha my knees turn to jelly.'

He gave her one of his rare smiles. People noticed and wondered what the young lady had said to entertain the marquess. Fenton Dantes noticed too, and he lifted his quizzing glass as he speculated.

Julia was glad she seemed to have lightened his mood. They danced well together. Holding hands with him now and then during the dance made her feel stupidly happy. She reminded herself that she must not speculate about him in a private way. His person, his status and their occasional meetings were not enough to qualify more than a passing alliance. She liked him enough to at least hope that she'd see him now and again in church if he were in resident at Cobham.

She expected to join her party when

the dance ended, but he led her to a narrow alcove on the other side of the room. 'My mother and my sister are here too. My mother particularly said she'd like to meet you again one day. She will be pleasantly surprised to see you here this evening.'

Unable to resist and suitably surprised, Julia followed without resistance. She bobbed when they reached the group with Lady de Vere seated in the middle.

'Good evening, Miss Stratton. I am surprised to see you here this evening. I was not aware that you were in London.'

'I am visiting my aunt and uncle. My friend's parents are kind enough to include me in their party. They are here for the season. We met Mr Grenville a couple of days ago and I suspect that he asked his sister to send us an invitation. I confess it has been very enjoyable so far.'

She nodded. 'And when will you be returning home?'

'I'm leaving in two weeks' time. My

friend and her parents will be here for two months longer.'

'And do you regret that you won't be with them?'

'No, I have had a very agreeable visit. My aunt and uncle are extremely kind, and my friend's parents include me in all their excursions. I am not greedy. When I return I will have a lot of pleasant memories. I am also sure that my mama misses me and is looking forward to my return.'

Lady de Vere looked at her speculatively for a moment and turned to her daughter. 'Charlotte, I think it would be pleasant to invite Miss Stratton to join us for dinner one evening, don't you? With her aunt and uncle, of course.'

Charlotte looked surprised for an instant before she looked at Julia and smiled. 'Of course, Mama! It will be a pleasure.'

Julia had no way of politely declining. She was sure it was an invitation that would produce agitation in her relations.

'Good! Then I look forward to seeing you, Miss Stratton. My daughter will be in touch as soon as we have consulted our engagement diary.'

Julia bobbed, and the marquess offered his arm to conduct her back to her party on the other side of the room. When they were out of hearing, he leaned and whispered, 'You have impressed my mother. It is not often that I have heard her offer a spontaneous invitation to anyone.'

'Then I'm honoured. But I am not sure that it is wise, and I certainly don't understand why she has done so.'

'She clearly thinks that if Hugh has offered you his friendship, you must be worth knowing. She has never told him so, but she likes Hugh a great deal; and if Hugh approves of you, she is also prepared to give you her seal of approval.'

'Oh! I see. I knew it would be ill-mannered to refuse, so I must resign myself to feeling grateful.'

He looked sideways and his smile

flashed briefly before he commented. 'Just remember your aunt up in Scotland. My mother can be daunting; but if you can endure your aunt, I'm sure that you will survive a dinner party with my mother.'

She looked down and began to laugh softly. He rewarded her with a courteous smile again and delivered her back to the party. They were sitting, agog to hear about her conversation with such illustrious persons. Julia didn't mention the invitation in case it was just a passing politeness.

7

The invitation did arrive, and as expected it sent her aunt into a flurry. She stated she had nothing suitable to wear, and her dressmaker would not have enough time to make something new.

Julia's aunt remarked, 'Your pale yellow dress with the embroidered hem will be perfect; it goes well with your dark colouring. But what can I wear on such an occasion?

Julia laughed. 'Dear Aunt! You have plenty of suitable gowns. Your dark green silk with ribbon piping suits you perfectly, and your beautiful cashmere shawl will be a delightful contrast. I think that will do very well, but you have other gowns that suit too. We are not dining with the King, are we?'

'True, but they are a noble family and it is a great honour they bestow on you. I recall how you told me about the marquess's accident near the cottage and the invitation to the picnic later, but quite honestly my love, I didn't think you'd hear any more. I presumed his visit was a one-off way of expressing thanks.'

'That's what I thought too. But Mr Grenville and the marquess are very good friends, and the marquess knows Mr Grenville has singled us out for attention once or twice. Perhaps that has something to do with it. The marquess did mention that his mother approved of anyone that Mr Grenville favoured. She has signed the invitation personally, so she does expect us to attend.'

Her aunt fiddled with the lace trimming on the neckline of her muslin dress. 'I have heard rumours that Lady de Vere is a very resolute character and that she doesn't suffer fools gladly.'

Julia viewed her and nodded. 'I have only met her twice. I get that impression too. She says what she thinks, but she also demonstrates understanding and sympathy.'

'I still think it is surprising that she pays you such attention. Her interest has nothing to do with your uncle or myself.'

Julia shrugged. 'I agree it is unexpected, but there is no reason for you or me to feel inferior. I've met them before and none of them made me feel uncomfortable.'

'Well, I must admit I am greatly nervous about the whole thing. I will send an immediate acceptance, of course — what else can I do? But I am still very apprehensive.'

Julia patted her arm. 'Don't be. It is likely only to be a family dinner, and I don't think any of them would be outright rude to their guests. They are too cultivated to do that. We can withdraw in a timely fashion, perhaps when the gentlemen join us later?'

'Your uncle will probably feel more comfortable. He often has to do with families of great standing, so he knows how to converse and become involved.'

Julia's laugh was hearty and intentional. 'Oh, Aunt! Stop worrying. Everything will be well. If anyone tries to treat me rudely, I will respond accordingly. That is one thing that is reassuring — I can now afford to speak truthfully. So can you.'

* * *

Three days later, her uncle's coach drew up outside the marquess's house in Courtland Street. After she and her aunt had descended, she looked up at the imposing façade. Her aunt gave Julia a meaningful glance. Her uncle noticed her appraisal too and merely patted her hand. Their arrival had brought the butler to open the door. He bowed as the party reached the entrance.

'Good evening, sir, madam, miss. May I take your garments?' He waited and handed the items to a second servant standing at his side. 'Will you please follow me? The family is in the red drawing room.' He walked ahead, his back as stiff as a ramrod. He announced them and withdrew.

After the introductions and greetings were completed, Lady de Vere said, 'Gareth, will you offer our guests something to drink?'

Gareth complied. Julia's uncle took a glass of Madeira and the two ladies took crystal goblets of lemonade. Lady de Vere gestured to a chair at her side and invited Julia's aunt to take a seat. Her aunt looked very nervous at first, but Julia could tell Lady de Vere was trying to put her at her ease, and she sighed with relief. Her uncle was soon in conversation with the marquess's sister and her husband. It was left up to the marquess to entertain Julia.

He stood at her side, and she had the feeling he was searching to something suitable to say. Julia cut him short. 'It is all right, your lordship. Please don't worry about trying to entertain me. I am perfectly happy to stand here and sip from my glass. We don't need to converse about trivialities.'

The corner of his mouth twitched as he viewed her. 'I would be a bad host if I just stood next to our guests all evening without saying a word, wouldn't I?'

'As long as you and your guests are happy, why not? I have no doubt that you would rather be elsewhere this evening, but it was very kind of your mother to invite us.'

'Ever since my mother heard you were in London, she expressed the wish to see you again, Miss Stratton. I think you impressed her that day you came to the picnic. The majority of young women she meets are not quite so . . . How can I put it without sounding rude . . . '

'Direct, perhaps? Outspoken?'

He touched his nose with a lace handkerchief and his eyes twinkled. Julia ploughed on. 'I assure you that my mother doesn't approve of my candour either, but I enjoy saying what I think. I no longer have to guard my behaviour so closely. I hope I am never rude, but I admit it is very agreeable not to have to pretend. The majority of young women of my age are expected to do the accepted thing, unless of course they are exceptionally rich, and not yet married.'

Without comment he changed the subject. 'Before I forget, I must mention that I enquired into who owns those ramshackle houses in the village. I discovered that I know their owner very well. His son and I went to university together. I suggested he should take a look at the place, and he did. I met him at the club yesterday. I think he was quite put out by what he saw. He has instructed his agent to put things in a decent order.'

Julia's colour rose. 'Really? That was very good of you, sir. I am so pleased! I had no means of improving their lot other than the occasional gift of some vegetables and the like, but everyone should have decent housing if they pay rent. I know that your estate is well run and your tenants do not face such conditions, but I did not dream you would involve yourself in such a way. Thank you!'

He tipped his chin. 'I honestly think Johnson didn't know about the state of the place. If you have a bad agent, things like that can happen.' After a short pause, he continued, 'Dr Dutton mentioned you are thinking of teaching the children reading and writing?'

'Yes, though I don't know if we will be able to persuade the parents yet. A number of children always attend Dr Dutton's children's service on Sunday afternoon. I thought that I could use their visit to teach them the rudiments. He says he would shorten his children's service by half an hour to give me a little time to do so. I know that the children from the ramshackle houses are interested. I have drawn letters in the ground for them. They try to copy, and are thirsty for more.'

He eyed her wordlessly and then commented, 'Undoubtedly it's a very commendable idea.'

'Well, the children will never get the

chance of any schooling otherwise. Most of the parents don't see the necessity. Most of them expect the children to help them in whatever they have to do themselves during the week, even if it is just sitting in a field all day looking after the farmer's geese.'

Gareth fingered his glass, and his signet ring glistened from the light of the sconces on the nearby walls. 'I presume you haven't considered that some people think schooling for the poorer classes is dangerous? That it breeds rebellion?'

'What's dangerous about being able to write your own name, or read some kind of proclamation on the wall? It can only help to improve someone's abilities.'

He put down his glass and straightened his wristbands. 'Miss Stratton, that is what a lot of landowners fear!'

The butler entered at that moment and announced, 'Mr Hugh Grenville, Lord and Lady Wilburton, Miss Charlotte Dandridge and Lord Kildare.'

Julia watched the party as they went to greet Lady de Vere. At her side still, the marquess commented, 'You seem to like Hugh?'

'Yes, I do. He has been extremely kind to me ever since I met him. He's a real gentleman. He mentioned that you and he are the best of friends.'

The marquess viewed Hugh as he stopped to exchange a few words with Julia's uncle. 'Yes, Hugh is a capital fellow.'

Smiling, Hugh came towards them, bowed briefly to Julia, and smiled at his friend. 'What a pleasure. I didn't expect to see you here this evening, Julia.'

The butler returned to announce the arrival of Lord and Lady Wainbridge and their daughter, Felicity. She was a beautiful redhead with emerald eyes, and she immediately came across to sweetly claim the marquess's attention. Clearly they hadn't met for the first time, and her laughter soon rang out across the room as they stood in a niche deep in conversation.

Julia viewed them while asking Hugh what he'd been doing since they'd last met. She wondered if she was looking at the future marchioness. For some reason she didn't like the idea.

The butler announced that dinner was served. Hugh held out his arm. 'May I have the pleasure of leading you to the dinner table?'

'Thank you! I would like that.'

They set off to follow some of the others who were already on their way to the dining room. Lady de Vere got up and waited for her son to relinquish Miss Wainbridge to a friend of his brother-in-law's. 'Sometimes everyone seems to forget the correct protocol. They all know that you and I should lead the way, Gareth.'

He viewed the departing silhouettes of Julia and Hugh. 'Things are changing, Mama. And this is a family dinner. We are not entertaining the Lord Mayor.'

His mother noticed that his eye was fixed on his friend and Julia. 'Hugh seems very taken with Miss Stratton. It would not be an appropriate match, of course, but she is an unusual girl and I can understand why he likes her. I don't think she will ever be prepared to be a light-skirt, so I imagine Hugh is going to be disappointed.'

The marquess straightened slightly and offered her his arm. 'Yes, I've already told him so. I expect he is disappointed that nothing can come of it. He clearly likes her, and I can understand that. Shall we?'

* * *

The evening was more than pleasant than Julia expected. She was next to Hugh at the dinner table, while her aunt was between Lord and Lady Wilberforce, who seemed to be doing their best to converse with her between the various courses. Her uncle was down the table, near the marquess at the top of the table. Lady de Vere faced him at the bottom. The others were seated in the remaining places. Miss Wainbridge was seated near the marquess, and they continued to exchange conversation animatedly whenever possible.

Hugh was his usual self and asked about Amelia. 'I hope she is well?'

'Thank you; yes, very well. Since your sister was kind enough to invite us that evening, we have received several invitations to attend other assemblies and soirées. Amelia's mother is delighted.'

'And where will they be this evening?'

'They are engaged to go to the theatre. I believe Garret is playing in a tragedy. I expect I will hear all about the tear-evoking story tomorrow when I see Amelia. She is delightfully emotional and takes everything to heart.'

'Yes, she is very charming.' He hastened to add, 'And you are too, in a completely different way.' He asked casually, 'Where are you engaged to go next week? Do you know?'

Julia managed to recall some invitations Amelia's mother had selected for the coming week, including a masked ball. 'I believe I have an invitation for some of those evenings as well. Now that I know you will be there, it will encourage me to attend them too.' She considered him for a moment. 'I am sure Amelia will be delighted to see you again . . . and I will too, of course.'

Later, the ladies were asked to perform some music when the men rejoined them. Julia was persuaded to sing, and Lady Wilburton agreed to accompany her. They were both middling performers, but their audience appreciated their efforts. Hugh gave a rousing rendition of a military marching song and Juliet found he had a pleasant tenor voice. Her aunt and uncle were persuaded to sing a duet and they sounded very harmonious. The party then broke into groups to play cards or just to gossip.

Julia preferred reading to cards, so she picked up a book lying on a nearby table, and was about to examine it closer when Lady de Vere came to sit next to her.

'Are you enjoying London, Miss Stratton?'

'Yes, very much.' Julia mused that her stern demeanour and bearing probably made some people hesitant to hold a normal conversation with her, but she herself had no such inhibitions. 'I presume you have attended so many seasons that you now find it almost boring?'

Lady de Vere flicked her fan open. There was a flash of amusement in her expression. 'Well, yes. I'm afraid that it does sometimes seem tedious after so many years, but I can still very well remember the time when I was young and enjoyed dancing and meeting new faces. I met my husband in the first London season I attended.'

'I believe that is still one of the main intentions behind it. It has always been an unofficial marriage market, hasn't it? It gives everyone a chance to meet a large number of people from all walks of life. People they would normally never encounter.'

Her dark eyes were piercing and questioning. 'And have you met anyone in this 'marriage market' yet'?'

Julia laughed. 'I am not looking, your ladyship. I think I told you that before. I am quite satisfied with my lot. I do not need, or intend, to accept the security of marriage to a rural presbyter or to a rustic gentleman twice my age! I think I can lead a more comfortable life on my own.'

Lady de Vere gave her the inklings of a smile. 'Yes, I remember our conversation that day at Cobham very well.' She looked up, and her glance halted at the table where Hugh and the marquess were playing cards with his sister's husband and Charlotte Dandridge. Absentmindedly she commented, 'I am hoping this season will bear fruit and our family will be able to announce a happy event soon. It is high time.'

Julia followed the direction of her eyes and guessed she was referring to her son's betrothal, perhaps with her daughter's friend or Miss Wainbridge. Probably there were others; undoubtedly he was the catch of the season if he was looking for a wife. Julia didn't comment and asked no questions. Somehow she didn't want to think of it. She had barely exchanged ten sentences with Charlotte Dandridge, and she hadn't been officially introduced to Felicity Wainbridge. She wasn't well acquainted with the marquess either, so she wasn't equipped to imagine who would suit as the future Marchioness de Vere. 'I'm sure your family and all society will be delighted if the marquess declares he has found someone he intends to marry.'

With a swish of her fan, Lady de Vere uttered, 'Society has been waiting long enough, and so have we.'

'Perhaps the marquess is hoping to find someone who not only has the right social standing but who also makes him happy.'

The older woman stared at her closely. 'Has he told you that?'

'No, I don't know his lordship well enough to be in his confidence about his private life. And I do think he is a very private person. I merely meant that the majority of couples marry either for social standing or for reasons of financial gain. Many ignore, or are persuaded to ignore, the aspect of personal happiness. His lordship is in the fortunate position of being able to choose his bride. Why should he not hope for happiness as well as matrimonial fulfilment? I presume that you want him to be happy.'

Lady de Vere's eyes widened. 'You are very outspoken, young woman!'

Julia coloured. 'Yes, I am. Forgive me if I offend you, your ladyship. I tend to forget my place and that I should hold my tongue. I overstep the mark constantly these days, because I am not beholden to anyone except my mother. Your family is no concern of mine. But you can be sure that I wish you, your son, and your family every happiness.'

After a second of silence, the older woman tapped Julia's knee with her fan. 'I know it was well meant, child. I take no offence. My son mentioned you are thinking of teaching some children from the village to read and write.'

Julia was glad to change the subject, and they chatted about what was involved and how much success or how much opposition she was likely to encounter. Julia noticed the marquess glanced in their direction sometimes with a puzzled expression. He was probably worried that she might be annoying his mother.

* * *

It was quite late when the Lady de Vere declared she was tired. It preceded a general approval to break up. Juliet happened to catch the marquess' eye when she did so. With a blank expression, he raised his eyebrows and gave her a knowing look. She smiled back. Gradually she was beginning to realize that under his outward mask of rigidity and control he had a sense of humour, and she'd always liked that in a man. She decided that she liked him too much for her own good.

On the way home, her aunt oozed satisfaction and enthused over how pleasant everyone had been. 'Not a sign of arrogance or smugness. Lady de Vere even complimented me on my dress and asked the name of my dressmaker.'

Julia was glad it had gone off so well. It was a memory to store away for the time when she was back home in Witheringston with Mama again.

* * *

The following week everyone they met was pleased that the number of balls and assemblies were increasing. Amelia's mother was delighted about the attention Amelia had received so far. Several young men had sent her small posies as a sign of their admiration, and Julia had also received a very pretty posy of yellow roses from an anonymous sender. Amelia thought it was very romantic because it was anonymous, and spent time every evening viewing the young men present and speculating who had sent it to her friend.

Julia didn't waste any time thinking about it. In her opinion, anyone who chose to remain anonymous wasn't worth consideration.

They often met Hugh at the same events; sometimes with just one friend, other times with several. One evening the marquess was part of his group. Someone caught his attention on the other side of the room as soon as they came in, so he dipped his chin in acknowledgement when he caught their attention. Amelia's eyes brightened and she blushed becomingly when Hugh joined their party.

Julia also recognized with pleasure a familiar face: John Fellows. He was a former friend of her brother's, and captain with the dragoons. He was standing among a group of soldiers in one of the corners. They drew the attention of all the single young ladies in the room, and the soldiers were fully aware of the effect they were having.

Julia wondered what it was about a uniform that attracted females like bees to pollen. Probably it had to do with heroics, as the Battle of Waterloo was still fresh in everyone's minds.

John had attended university with her brother and then joined the militia. He'd survived Waterloo; but as he was not likely to inherit much, a military career was the most attractive possibility for someone like him who had to make his way in the world as best he could. He was very tall and slim and had corn-coloured hair and blue eyes. He stopped in his tracks when he saw Julia and hurried over, looking delighted.

She smiled and held out her hand. 'John! What are you doing here?'

He grinned, kissed the back of her palm and said, 'I could ask you the same question! What a pleasure to see you among so many strange faces. I'm on leave and I plan to depart for home in a few days' time. I'm going to visit my parents and the rest of the family. In fact, I was intending to call to see you and your mother on the way there.'

'Oh, please do! Mama will be so delighted to see you again. Like old times.'

He said quietly, 'Not quite like old times though, is it? I miss knowing that Richard is not at Fallowdean anymore. It was such bad luck, his fall. Bad luck for him, and for you and your mother when your father died so soon after. I was at a new posting in the north of England and didn't hear about both events until weeks later. I would have tried to get special leave to attend the funerals. I liked your father, and Richard was my best friend and a good fellow.'

With misty eyes, she patted his arm. 'I know. Mama kept your kind letters. We didn't know where to reach you when Papa died. Your regiment had moved, and in the pandemonium of leaving Fallowdean I didn't have time to make enquiries. I hope you forgive me. It was not my intention to exclude you from hearing of Papa's death in a timely fashion.'

'I heard anyway. You'd be surprised how news travels sometimes.'

She gestured to her party. 'I'd like to introduce you to my friends, John. They have included me in their arrangements ever since they came to London. I think you met Amelia a couple of times at Fallowdean, didn't you?'

He nodded and bowed. Once the introductions were over, John danced with both women; and when Hugh came with the marquess, Julia noticed a fleeting look of irritation when the former saw Amelia in the arms of the good-looking young officer.

They exchanged floccules with everyone until John returned with Amelia on his arm. Hugh still had to be patient because another gentleman had been promised the next dance. He tried to appear unconcerned, but Julia could tell by the way his eyes followed her on the dance floor that Hugh was in danger of falling in love with her friend.

John asked her to dance, and as they circled the floor and he chatted about his duties in the north, she had time to think about Hugh and Amelia. Amelia did not have the same social standing as Hugh, but she was genteel enough, and her parents were rich. Hugh would not inherit a title or many possessions, but he owned a small manor house in Sussex and received a small annual income from an inheritance from an uncle. He had two older brothers, so he had little to expect from his parents. Julia began to wonder if an attachment between the two was possible. She thought Amelia had had a tendre for Hugh for some time, and she understood why. They suited each other; and if they did fall in love, what could be more appropriate or better for them both?

After John brought her back, he bowed and took his leave, promising that when his plans were set, he would let her know when he would be calling at the cottage.

Hugh asked Amelia to dance. The marquess had little choice but to ask

Julia to dance as well, and she accepted. She always felt strangely comfortable in his presence and was glad that he did not continually chatter as a lot of men did. He was clearly a private man. By now she was sure she did like him. After a few minutes he asked about John, and she obliged him by explaining the connection. 'He wrote a lovely letter after he heard of Richard's death. He was unable to attend the funeral. It's very kind of him not to forget us. He intends to call on his way to visiting his own family. My mother will be delighted to see him, I'm sure.'

The marquess nodded. A moment later she noticed a sudden change in his countenance, and soon realized the reason was that Fenton Dantes had appeared on the fringe of the dance floor. He stood with his pince-nez focused on the dancers, and it lingered on the marquess and Julia until the music ended.

On their way back to Amelia and the others, he crossed their path. With a sweeping bow, he said, 'Good evening,

Miss Stratton. Good evening, de Vere.'

The marquess viewed him silently with thin lips. It was clear he bore the man no affection. Julia thought someone had to say something. 'Good evening, Mr Dantes!'

'Is your dance card filled, Miss Stratton? If not, I would like the pleasure.'

The marquess said coldly, 'I thought you disliked dancing, Fenton. You're usually only interested in the ladies on the cards at the gambling tables.'

Fenton smirked and his eyes glittered dangerously. 'Then that shows that you don't know me very well. Who could ever resist dancing with someone as attractive as Miss Stratton, if given the chance?'

Julia hastened to do what she could to calm the atmosphere. 'I regret, Mr Dantes, but I have none free anymore.'

Fenton Dantes bowed again. 'My loss, dear lady. Perhaps another time.' With a barely perceptible nod to Gareth, he turned and disappeared into the crowd.

Julia had lied in pretending her card

was full. She felt uneasy in Dantes's presence. It was probably because the two men were clearly so hostile to each other; but it also had to do with his black clothing, piercing eyes, long fingers and sycophantic manner.

The marquess did not comment, and returned her to the Wilcox party. He asked Amelia for the next dance, and she was too much in awe of his title to refuse him, although some ill-fated youth whose name was written in for that dance was left high and dry. Amelia's mother frowned and had the unpleasant task of persuading the youth that there must be some kind of mix-up.

Julia had promised the dance to someone too, so when the dance ended and she returned, she found herself standing next to the marquess. He stood silently. Julia was silent too. All of them watched Hugh dancing with Amelia. When they returned, both of them smiling, the marquess said something quietly in his friend's ear, and soon after they took their leave.

Julia watched the two men as they

left and hoped that she wasn't imagining things. She would never forgive the marquess if he interfered between Hugh and her dear friend. Hugh was definitely one of her admirers. Julia honestly hoped the two of them would find out what they felt for each other without any outside interference or advice — especially not from someone like the marquess, who was so caged in by protocol that he wouldn't be able to imagine that personal feeling could take precedent over social demands.

8

The next morning, the two women mused that as Julia's departure was fixed, they had two weeks left in which to decide what they still wanted to do and see before she left. Amelia was changing into a walking dress when Julia arrived. She waited for her in the sitting room. Mrs Wilcox was imploring her to stay in London a little longer, but Julia resisted the temptation.

'Mama has been alone long enough. I expect she is longing to hear all the latest news. Amelia doesn't need my support any longer, Mrs Wilcox. She is the belle of the ball wherever she goes, and I am sure that will continue when the season is in full swing.'

Fanny Wilcox smiled. 'Yes, she is doing well, isn't she? I wouldn't be surprised if she receives an offer before it is out.'

'Yes, I think you may be right.'

'Where are you planning to go this morning?'

'We are going to walk through the park and then to Wigmore Street to the draper's. Amelia wants some blue ribbon to trim her straw bonnet, and we want to purchase masks for the fancy ball on Wednesday.'

'Oh, yes. Mr Wilcox and I still have ours from the last time we were in London. They are rather ramshackle now, but no one will look at us twice anyway. If you can, Julia, try to persuade Amelia to buy a mask that matches her dress, in dusky pink or pink and white. And she needs a few ostrich feathers for her headdress too.'

Amelia returned, and thankfully that saved Julia the bother of promising Mrs Wilcox anything. The colour of their masks presented no problem, but Amelia would be in dudgeons if she had to wear ostrich feathers. For some reason, she disliked them greatly.

Mrs Wilcox smiled at them. 'If you

are going through the park, the footman can go with you.'

Anticipating this, Julia had already made arrangements. 'My aunt's maid, Maggie, has come with me, ma'am. My aunt always makes sure I do not go alone anywhere. She insisted Maggie accompany me here, and if necessary remain with us on our outing this morning.'

'Oh very well, but be careful. Talk to no strangers, girls! Where is this Maggie?'

'She is waiting out in the hallway.'

'Very well, be off then and try to be punctual for luncheon. The cook is trying a new asparagus recipe, and I would like to hear what you think of it.'

Nodding, the two young women hastened to escape. Julia warned Amelia that Maggie would soon start to complain. She did five minutes later, declaring that she was fagged to death. Julia was used to Maggie's complaints by now; she knew they were generally a lot of hot air.

It was a beautiful morning and the

park was busy. They had the satisfaction of acknowledging several people they met along the way. Gradually some people recognized their faces from the assemblies and various other entertainments they'd attended. They walked through the park towards the exit on the opposite side.

Julia's good mood was dampened when she noticed a black figure strolling towards them. Another man was at his side. She recognized Fenton Dantes even at a distance, and drew Amelia's attention to him.

With a sidelong glance at Julia, but keeping her head still, Amelia said, 'I do not like him much, Julia.'

Julia avoided direct eye contact with the two men as they drew closer, and said quietly, 'Marquess de Vere may be related to Dantes, but he's hostile towards him whenever they meet; and when I mentioned him to my aunt, she said if he was the same Fenton Dantes she'd heard of, he has a bad reputation and is a bit of a gamester. He dresses very elegantly and appears to be of the first *ton*, but he's always in black. Personally I find that's morbid or sinister. He probably wants to impress the world and stand out. I have never noticed the least generosity in his disposition, and I confess I cannot warm to him. I try hard to keep an open mind because he has given me no reason to dislike him.'

Amelia nodded but remained silent as they drew alongside.

Fenton lifted his high top hat. 'Good morning, ladies. What a pleasure! My friend and I are on our way to visit an acquaintance who lives near here.' He indicated his friend. 'This is Mr Freddy Maldon. Freddy, these are two young ladies who are fast becoming the toast of the town — Miss Julia Stratton and Miss Amelia Wilcox.'

Fenton's friend was rather portly. He wore a high collar that was causing him to look and feel uncomfortable. He eyed them and bowed. He viewed Julia briefly, but his glance rested on Amelia longer than politeness allowed, and Amelia unconsciously pulled nervously at the strings of her purse when she noticed. 'No doubt you are out enjoying the sunshine?'

Julia met his question with assurance. 'Yes, but we are just about to leave the park. We have some items to procure in Bedford House.'

He tipped the brim of his hat. 'Then we will keep you no longer. I hope to see you at Lady Mablethorpe's fancy ball on Wednesday?'

Julia wished she could answer differently. 'Probably.'

He nodded. 'Well, good morning, ladies, and enjoy your shopping expedition.' He viewed Maggie in the background. 'I see that you are suitably accompanied. Good! Young ladies shouldn't be at the mercy of any unsuitable persons, here or any other part of London.'

They parted company, and Julia was glad to be on the move again.

* * *

Julia joined the Wilcoxes early the day of the fancy ball. The ladies enjoyed getting ready. It was not a costume ball with complete fancy dress, but those attending were expected to at least wear a mask with their evening dress. Amelia and Julia let Amelia's maid curl and dress their hair in such a way that they hoped made them look different. They wore half-masks and thought they had a good chance of not being recognized until the unmasking at eleven. They'd had great difficulty in persuading Mrs Wilcox that she should not sit by them all evening.

'If you do that, Mama, everyone will know straight away who we are. We have spoken with several other ladies, and they are going to ask their parents or guardians to sit on the opposite side of the room. You will still be able to see us.'

Her mother threw her hands up in the air and sighed. 'I think it is a very silly idea. Anyone who knows you will recognize you.'

Amelia begged, 'Oh, don't protest so, Mama. It will be so much fun if we can befog someone.'

'Do not use such expressions, Amelia. No lady would use that kind of language.'

Amelia lifted her eyes to heaven and her friend smiled.

Eventually her daughter persuaded her there was no harm in their idea, and Amelia, her parents and Julia set off in the coach. When they arrived, the ballroom was already quite full, and the two young women left Amelia's parents in the hallway. They sought out two empty chairs among groups of twittering, high-voiced ladies sitting along the walls. They were trying to hide their identity behind their various masks and ornamentation.

The various rooms were very fine, especially the ballroom where the ladies sat. The light blue walls were ornamented with carvings and paintings. One large recess in the ballroom was entirely of looking-glass, and there was a profusion of wall sconces that illuminated the whole area, as well as a very large central lustre. The curtains, sofas and chairs were of blue silk with gold fringe. Julia and Amelia agreed that it was one of the richest assembly rooms they'd seen so far.

They also thought it very enjoyable not to dance strictly with who was listed on their dance cards. The younger male visitors clearly found the idea of asking an anonymous young lady to dance with them entertaining too, although the women were not as anonymous as they hoped they'd be. As the evening progressed, they saw that Amelia's parents had found their places at a small table on the opposite side of the room. Julia spotted them leaving the room together later and presumed that they were on their way to the refreshment in the adjoining room for tea, or Mr Wilcox was on his way to the card room.

After just a few minutes, a liveried servant approached them. 'Excuse me, ladies. Are you Miss Amelia Wilcox and Miss Julia Stratton?'

The girls looked at him in puzzlement and then replied simultaneously, 'Yes.'

'I am sorry to bear bad news, but Mrs Wilcox had been taken ill and Mr Wilcox has asked me to instruct you to come home immediately. He has gone ahead with his wife and has arranged for another coach to collect you in ten minutes, after you have retrieved your cloaks.'

Amelia paled and her hand covered her mouth. It was left to Julia to ask, 'What happened? What is wrong?'

'I cannot say, miss. I was only asked to bring you the message by the head porter. I did not see what was wrong with the lady.'

'But I saw them going for refreshments a few minutes ago!'

He shrugged and wrung his hands. 'I don't know about that, miss, but apparently the gentleman was very upset and begged that the message be delivered as soon as possible.'

Julia got up. 'I'll check, in case there is some kind of mistake.'

'The gentleman said it was extremely urgent, and he described exactly what you were wearing. I don't think there can be any doubt about it.'

Amelia clutched at Julia's arm. 'Oh, let us go, Julia! Every minute that we delay is too long. Poor Mama! I did not notice that she was off colour, but perhaps we've attended too many events recently, and it has brought on the vapours. I do hope it is nothing serious.' She bit her lip nervously.

'Oh, very well. Don't worry, Amelia. One of us would have noticed if she was fagged by all the goings-on. We'll collect our cloaks and find the coach your papa ordered for us.'

'It is already waiting, miss. If you follow me, I will help you find your cloaks.'

The two women hurried after him. Just as they were leaving, they saw Hugh arriving. He smiled at them. 'Just the ladies I hoped to find.'

Julia stalled any further conversation. 'Hugh, we must leave. Amelia's mother has been taken ill and we are just off.'

'Oh! Nothing serious I hope. Can I help?'

'No, we just received a message to come home. A coach is already waiting for us, so you must forgive us for leaving you like this.'

He nodded. 'Then I hope that it is a trifle. Sometimes a mere stomach upset can make one feel quite ill.'

Amelia looked at him but said nothing. She turned and followed Julia into the hallway. They soon found their cloaks, and the servant accompanied them to the entrance and pointed to a stately carriage waiting in the shadows. It had curtained windows on all sides. The coachman stood beside the open door, and Amelia hurried to climb the steps. Julia heard a slight flurry of movement as she disappeared inside. She was directly behind her friend and as she'd finished getting in, the coachman was already folding the steps and slamming the door. The carriage shook as he sprang onto the box to flick the reins, setting the horses off at a fast pace down the road.

They were not alone in the coach. There were also two dark figures with them. What was going on? Julia had no time to make any sense of it. In the semi-darkness her eyes had adjusted enough to see that one of them was Fenton Dantes, and he was holding a rag over Amelia's mouth. She slumped into his arms. At that moment someone put a cloth over her own mouth, and although she tried to struggle, she registered a faintly sweet smell and then sunk into black oblivion.

* * *

When she woke, Julia found that she and Amelia were lying on a large four-poster bed with dusty velvet curtains and a musty dark red bedcover. Amelia was still asleep.

Julia slipped her legs over the edge of the bed and tried to stand but found she was too giddy. She sat down again and looked around. The room was darkly panelled; indeed, everything in it seemed to be dark. The furniture was old and badly looked after, and covered in a layer of dust. There was a musty smell to the whole room and it was clearly seldom used. She figured they must have been asleep for hours, because the light coming through a pair of dark red velvet curtains was still pale and weak. It was probably near daybreak.

As her mind cleared, she remembered how Fenton Dantes and his friend had kidnapped them. It didn't seem rational. What for? She had no financial expectations, and Amelia's family weren't enormously rich either. Amelia's parents would pay a decent sum to get her back, but there must be a lot of other women who came from richer families who would present a better prospect. The whole thing was too well organized to be some kind of joke. They'd been deliberately drugged and abducted.

Holding on to the bedpost, Julia tried to stand again, and this time she felt sounder. Holding on to convenient pieces of furniture, she went towards the window and drew the curtains aside. It was not locked, and when she felt the cold air on her face, it swept away some of the wooziness. They were in some kind of large house. She leaned outside, looking along the length of what was probably a country manor house. The room was on the second level. Jumping to ground level would be too hazardous. Ivy grew all over the walls, and some of the climbers were as thick as her wrist. If she got a grip, she'd climb down using the ivy. Richard had dared her to climb trees when they were growing up, and she hadn't forgotten how. Her dress would be a bit of a handicap, but she'd cope.

She studied the surrounding country-side. There was not another building, village, or township in sight. The birds were already chirping in the hedgerows and trees. She looked back towards her sleeping friend. Amelia would never be able to climb down via the ivy. They had to find another means to escape. Leaving the window open, she returned to the bed and shook Amelia gently. 'Amelia! Wake up. Wake up!'

Amelia stirred and her eyes opened slowly. As she recalled what had happened, she looked around in fright and uttered quietly, 'Where are we, Julia? What's happened? Why did those men kidnap us?'

'I wish I knew. I've been trying to figure it out. It can't be for money. There are a number of other women who are richer with better connections than us. I'm not worth anything, and your parents aren't immensely rich, are they?'

Amelia's eyes were frightened and round like saucers. 'Julia, do you think they are going to sell us into a harem? I read a novel a week ago when that happened.'

Julia almost wanted to laugh, but the situation was too serious. 'No, I don't think we are going to end up in a harem, but perhaps the two men do have something similar in mind. I can't think of another reason.'

Amelia's hand shot to her mouth. 'Do you mean . . .?'

She nodded. 'It's possible. My aunt told me that Fenton Dantes was depraved, a gambler, and had a bad reputation. I begin to understand why the marquess dislikes him so much.' She paused. 'That could also be a reason. He may be doing it to annoy his cousin, because he knows we are acquainted with the marquess and also with Hugh. Perhaps he intends to frighten us and then let us go after all, to teach the marquess a lesson. But somehow I think he may have other intentions.'

Amelia's eyes started to fill with tears. 'I would rather die than give myself to them. They are detestable.'

'We have to escape. We'll bargain, win time, and refuse to be parted. If they try that, we must fight them in any way we can to stop them — scratching, punching, spitting, kicking, anything! Richard told me he got into a lot of trouble in school once because he pushed his fingers into someone's eyes in a fight, and the other boy gave up and was in great pain for some time. So stick your fingers in their eyes if they touch you!'

Amelia was getting more agitated by the minute. Julia wasn't surprised. Amelia hadn't had a brother; fighting was not part of her upbringing. They had no more time to talk, as they heard the key turning in the lock.

With a smirk on his face, Fenton came in. He locked the door from within and played with the key. 'Good morning, ladies! Awake already? I expect you are anxious to find out what the day will bring?'

Amelia moved closer to Julia, who took some slow, even breaths. 'What is this about Mr Dantes?' Julia demanded. 'Why have you abducted us and brought us here? Release us at once! Where is this place, by the way?'

He laughed throatily and grinned at her. 'You are too intelligent not to realize why you are here, Miss Stratton. I wouldn't take such a risk just for fun. We are deep in the countryside. A hunting box I own. No one lives nearby, so there is no point in you wasting energy trying to escape or scream.' His eyelids fell and he viewed them nonchalantly for a moment. 'I almost feel sorry for you both, because no one will want used wares when we return to society.'

Supressing her fear, Julia felt how the hair on the nape of her neck lifted and how her body broke out in a cold sweat. 'I've heard that you are depraved. What do you think will happen to you when we return to our families? You will be punished and shunned by decent society thereafter.'

A faint satanic smile hovered as his eyes travelled over their figures. 'Do you think I honestly care? I've been planning to go abroad for a while now. Unfortunately I have a couple of creditors who are making my life unpleasant, and I think I'll simply disappear for a couple of years.'

Amelia was rooted to the spot, and stood as close as she could to Julia. Her face was ashen, and Julia could feel her shaking.

Julia licked her lips. 'I still don't understand why us. If you need women to entertain you and your friend, I am sure you know where to find willing ones on the corner of a street somewhere in London. Some women would find it a great temptation to spend some time in a grand house with servants, and all for the usual payment — I assume you do have servants?'

'You mean Covent Garden nuns? That would be no fun, my dear. Too run of the mill. You and your friend are much more amusing. My friend can't wait to be alone with your friend. He took a great fancy to her that day we met in the park. As to servants, I only have an old hag of a woman looking after the place, and she doesn't even do that properly. I sent her packing after we arrived yesterday.'

Julia's eyes were overly bright. 'Why? I have no fortune, and you must realize I detest you. It wouldn't be all fun, believe me!'

He laughed unsmilingly. 'You have no idea how useless resistance would be. You can annoy me a little perhaps, but you won't be able to stop me.'

He took a step closer, and she froze, but then she straightened her spine and stood her ground. Her gloved fists clenched.

He said quietly, 'My friend is slightly off colour at the moment. He drank too much brandy after we arrived. When he wakes I will sort out the details with him, and then I will return with the happy news of our next meeting. There is nothing to eat in the kitchen except some milk and some stale cheese. Perhaps I'll give you some of that, if you behave. Or there's plenty of gin and brandy if you prefer.'

Julia thought desperately how she could protect Amelia. It wouldn't matter so much if she were dishonoured in some way, but it would be disaster for her friend. It would change Amelia's life completely, even if it were through no fault of her own.

Fenton was already turning back to the door. 'Let Amelia go and I promise I will not resist you,' Julia pleaded.

She heard Amelia's indrawn breath and felt her grab her arm. Her voice shook. 'No, Julia!'

Julia patted her arm and waited for Fenton's reaction. He turned swiftly and viewed her, frowning. 'What's that for a stupid plan? And what do you think my friend will say if I agreed to let her go? Not that the idea of your surrender isn't much more appealing than the alternative, of course.'

Keeping her voice under control, she uttered, 'I'm sure you can dupe him with some lie or other. If you let Amelia go before your friend wakes, you can tell him we were both trying to escape and she got away. Do you have a horse or a horse and carriage? I presume the coach from last night was hired?'

He nodded and stroked his chin. 'Yes, it was. There's a gig in the stable and a pony that the housekeeper used. Why should I provide transport?'

'Because if she set out on foot, he could catch up with her, and then the truth would come out. Amelia can manage a gig.'

He looked at Julia for a moment. 'I need a moment to think this out. I'm not sure it is worth the bother. My friend will explode if he wakes and she's gone, although I suppose I could lie convincingly.' He unlocked the door and left.

He had scarcely gone when Amelia laid her hand on her heart. 'I won't leave, Julia. I won't leave you alone with these men. I know I am not as brave as you, but I will not let you sacrifice yourself for me. I would never forgive myself if I left you to your fate with these beasts.'

Julia grabbed her shoulders. 'You *must* leave, if he accepts. Once you've gone, I will try to escape myself. The ivy creepers outside the window are quite strong. I will climb down that way. You know that Richard and I spent lots of time climbing trees. I'll manage, don't worry. My dress is a hindrance, but that can't be helped. If I manage to get away, I'll set out across the fields and keep going until I find a village or someone to help. You would fall down from the ivy and you won't manage to keep up with me. I am used to hijinks in the countryside. You must leave, Amelia, if he gives us the chance. Try to find a village, an inn, and ask for the local magistrate. You can relate what happened to us last night and how we were brought here against our will.'

'But we don't know where we are!'

'He mentioned a hunting-box, and usually people in the countryside know where the bigger houses are. If you tell them his name and that we were taken to his hunting-box, I bet they know where it is. Once you've done that, tell them you must return to London at once. I am sure your parents are full of anxiety and fear. As soon as I can, I will try to find a magistrate and tell him the same thing. I will get word to you or my aunt, and we will meet up again as soon as possible.'

Amelia bit her lip. 'I don't like it, Julia. If you don't get away . . . '

Julia managed a playful grin. 'I will, but I can only succeed if I know *you* are away. We can't escape together at the same time, but perhaps we can trick him if he accepts my offer.'

The two women spent some time going over details, and Julia could tell that Amelia was beginning to understand it was a slim chance, but their only one. Julia reminded her of how Fenton's friend looked and how things might be if she didn't escape.

They both tested the strength of the ivy creepers near the window after checking no one was in the courtyard. Amelia didn't feel quite so frightened, but she wasn't cheerful either.

A short time later the key rattled in

the lock again, and the women eyed each other warily.

Fenton came in and viewed Julia. 'I have your word that you will not resist?'

She nodded. 'I will do whatever you wish, without struggling. You have my word.'

'Right! It will be best when she leaves straight away. My friend is still jug-bitten. Once he wakes, it will be difficult to arrange anything. He will smell a rat if I try to keep him out of the way, or if he hears a carriage leaving. You will be able to see the gig going down the lane to the right. Then you will know I kept my side of the bargain.' Nodding at Amelia, he said, 'Come along, and make no noise. I will saddle the pony and gig for you. You look a pretty useless sort of woman! The stable is on the other side of the house. Drive straight down the lane and you will come to a road.'

Amelia looked at Julia, who gave her a quick hug. 'Be off with you, and drive carefully.'

Impatiently, he stood waiting. To Julia he said, 'I will be back directly, and then we can have a comfortable afternoon together.'

Her mouth was dry but she nodded. She watched her friend leave and heard Fenton lock the door. She was relieved. Even if her own plan failed, she had at least helped to give Amelia a chance of escape. She did not think for long. He would be back as soon as he had seen the gig depart. She hurried to the window and nearly tripped over Amelia's slippers, blessing her friend silently. She must have slipped out of them after Fenton arrived. They were both wearing thin evening slippers, and Amelia must have mused that Julia would soon need new foot covering if she was to travel any distance. She shoved them into her beaded reticule and hoped it wouldn't burst apart at the seams, then thanked providence that the stables were on the opposite side of the house and Fenton couldn't see her. There was no time to be lost.

9

Julia grabbed a chair and climbed onto the windowsill. Pushing the material of her dress behind her and keeping her purse out of the way, she grabbed some creepers and swung herself out and across. She tried to find a firm foothold as she gradually slithered and slipped and descended. She scratched her hands and ripped her dress but she made progress, and eventually she jumped the last couple of feet.

Gathering her dress and holding onto Amelia's slippers, she looked around and set off for a nearby field. She ran and found a gap in the hedge. Not pausing to look back, she saw there was a small coppice or forest not far away, and reasoned she had a better chance of evading Fenton there than if she tried to make her way across open fields. She ran, feeling the roughness of the ground, and panting as she went. She was not sure how far she was from the house now, but she had been lucky. After Fenton had sent Amelia on her way, Julia still had a few minutes' respite until he returned to the house and came upstairs to look for her.

The morning was advancing fast, and she was relieved to reach the edge of the wood. Pausing for a moment, she could tell the thicket was not visited often. Bushes and undergrowth everywhere looked wild and very untamed. She went on, climbing over fallen tree trunks and going deeper into the wilderness, trying not to leave an obvious trail and pushing branches and vegetation back to their original position if she could.

She needed somewhere to hide until Fenton's attempts to find her ceased. There was no point in thinking she could outrun him. He probably had at least one other horse in the stable, but a horse would be of little use here in the thick coppice. The untamed undergrowth sprouted thickly everywhere, and the crowns of the trees let little sunshine in to the ground and greenery below.

Julia caught her breath, and her gaze darted here and there as she held her aching side for a moment. She spotted a cluster of fallen trunks that leaned against and over each other. On closer inspection, she found there was a small cave-like space at its centre. It was just what she needed. Gathering some dried brushwood and greenery to conceal any gaps, she climbed inside with care and prayed that the whole thing wouldn't collapse on her. It was a sobering thought that if it did, no one would ever find her, and Mama would worry about what had happened to her for the rest of her life.

It was damp and cool, but Julia was content to recover her breath and think. The effects of whatever drug Fenton had used were still there, and she found that thinking made her tired and the lack of motion sent her to sleep. She had no idea how much later it was when she heard footfalls coming through the thicket in her direction. She held her breath. The voices grew louder.

'Fenton, this is completely mad. This place is like a jungle. The one driving the carriage must be miles away already, and the other one could have gone in any direction. Why in God's name are we wasting time in this place?'

Fenton Dantes's voice was angry and taciturn. 'They were cleverer than I thought. When they split up, they double their chances. The Stratton girl is not stupid. It goes to show what a woman is capable of if she has a brain. This place is a perfect hidey-hole. It's not far from the house.'

They were close enough for Julia to see the colour of their coats among the trees. Her stomach knotted and fright swept through her for a moment.

'Well, I've had enough. Let them go. What do you intend to do with them if you find them? The only way to stop them gabbing would be to make them cold, and I'll have no part in that.

Abducting them was entertaining, and it's a pity we didn't get our just reward, but now we must leave for the continent as fast as we can. If one of them finds a magistrate before we're out of the country, we'll end up in Newgate Prison. This business, on top of our gambling debts, will finish us off. I'm going, and to devil with the girls! Are you coming or not?'

Fenton didn't reply, but Julia could see through the slits in the brushwood and hear him thrashing the surrounding ferns and undergrowth with a stick or sword. She flinched. Finally he said, 'Very well! I'm not cork-brained. I know that we're in trouble. Let us be off. There's no time for packing or getting our stuff from London. We just take what we brought with us last night. We're purse-pinched, so once we're in France we'll set up a card game or find a willing widow. Then we'll be able to make proper plans again.'

Julia lay still and waited. Her breathing was shallow and her heart was pounding in her ears. She heard them scrambling back through the wood, and continued to wait until she could hear nothing more except the sound of birds in the undergrowth. Breathing deeply with relief, she had to hold herself in check not to scramble out straight away. The slightest noise could attract Fenton back; the slightest sound from the wood.

After a while, she crept out and sat on a tree trunk. It must be early afternoon but she waited a little longer, comforted by the silence and the sounds of nature. She was hungry and very thirsty, and she busied herself with thinking about the past weeks. She hoped that Amelia had managed to get to safety. Then she found herself thinking about the marquess. How ridiculous! He lived on the moon, and she was an earth-dweller.

She decided at last to leave her hiding place and find a secure haven elsewhere. It took several minutes to reach the edge of the wood, and after a careful check that no one was in sight she set out across the adjoining field. She could not see Fenton's hunting-box, so she must be on another side of the coppice.

Her evening slippers were in tatters. The soles were thin, so she discarded them for Amelia's. One field bordered the next, only divided by straggly hedges. Julia had almost given up finding any trace of human beings when she spotted the outlines of a small cottage at the corner of a field. As she drew closer, she saw it was also positioned near a road. She hurried on. The house was a poor structure, and the roof needed repair, but there was smoke coming out of the chimney. Her optimism increased. Julia approached and took her courage in her hand to knock on the rough door. A middle-aged woman with clothes that needed washing opened it. She was shocked when she saw Julia.

'What do you want? Who are you? Be off with you — I'll have nothing to do with gipsies or vagrants.'

Julia knew she must look dreadful. Her dress was tattered and torn; it was dirty and little remained of its silk finery. Her hair was hanging around her face in untamed bits and pieces; and she felt, and probably looked, exhausted.

'Please, help me! My name is Julia Stratton. I have to speak with a magistrate or a policeman.' The woman stared at her as if bewitched. 'A man, Fenton Dantes, tried to keep me in his house. He intended to ruin me, but I managed to escape. How far is the next town?' She looked around. 'I don't suppose you have a horse or a donkey I could borrow? I promise I will see it is returned to you.' Her mouth was dry and her head was beginning to spin. 'Please can you give me some water? I am terribly thirsty! I have no money I can give you now, but I will reward you later, I promise.'

'Hmph! And crows will fly.'

Julia remembered the half crown the marquess had given her. She always had it with her, as she'd put it in her purse as a memento. She rummaged frantically and found it, then held it towards the woman. 'This is all I have, but I promise you more if you will help.'

The woman took the coin and looked at her carefully. 'All right. Sit there! I will get you some water. My husband will return soon and I will let him decide what we should do.'

'Thank you.' Julia sat down on a boulder next to the entrance door. The woman had barely gone inside when the world began to twirl and twirl faster until darkness descended, and she fell to the side in a faint.

* * *

The next thing she noticed was that she was in a carriage jostling along a country road. Her sight was still blurry, but she guessed it wasn't Fenton's carriage because her face rested on the soft thigh of someone wearing suede riding breeches. Someone held a silver flask to her lips and she obediently took a sip. As the liquid slid down her throat she didn't particularly like the taste, but it warmed her. She made an effort to struggle and sit up.

A firm hand on her shoulder held her in position and a familiar voice said, 'Stay where you are, Miss Stratton. When I found you, you were completely dehydrated; and although we managed to get some water and milk inside you, it takes time for the body to readjust. It happened to me once a long time ago. I fell down an old pit shaft and it took a while till someone found me.'

Her mouth felt furry but she continued to struggle. 'Your lordship! How did you find me? Heavens! I know I am dirty and extremely messy. I will ruin your clothes or your carriage.' Her sight was clearing fast and she looked up into his face.

A faint smile hovered round his mouth. 'True, I have seen you looking more comely, but don't fret about damage from a little dirt. My man will undoubtedly restore my apparel to its usual pristine appearance in no time at all, and the carriage doesn't matter.'

Julia concentrated her attention on the carriage's roof as he spoke.

'As to how I found you . . . Hugh and I had been searching all night, and so was your military friend. Hugh found out something was badly amiss soon after you disappeared in the coach. He met Amelia's parents after you'd left, and as soon as they realized something was very wrong, the search began. The servant could describe one of the men well enough for us to figure out who was in the coach. Hugh enquired discreetly, of course, and then he came to me because he thought I would know where to find Fenton.

'We tried his London address and his usual haunts, and then I remembered he had a hunting-box. When we set out to fetch our vehicles, we met John Fellows. I decided that as he knew you, he was the right kind of man to help us in our search, so I told him what had happened and he insisted on joining us. No one apart from us three and Miss Wilcox's parents know what has happened. We decided Fenton's hunting-box was a good bet — he doesn't have any other property.'

With eyes misting over, Julia asked weakly, 'Amelia?'

'She is safe. She found an inn, and the innkeeper roused the local magistrate. When we arrived, Hugh contacted the same magistrate to inform him, and he told Hugh where to find Miss Wilcox as she had just left. After she explained how she escaped and what you were planning do, Fellows and I continued searching for you while Hugh took Miss Wilcox back to London. We found that people locally have no love of Fenton. We checked that no one was at his house, and then split up in order to explore the immediate countryside. He started riding the fields. It was pure chance that I was driving down the road when a fellow stopped my carriage and said some woman had called at his cottage and was now dying next to his doorway.'

Julia could not help smiling a little. 'How dramatic!'

'The whole thing is quite theatrical.' He paused for a moment and asked in a quiet voice, 'I hope Fenton did not . . . ?' She shook her head and he nodded quickly. 'Good! Thank God for that. I sent the man to look for your friend and send him back to London. How did you escape?'

'After I climbed down the ivy and got away, I ran to a nearby wood. I waited there until I was sure he wasn't searching for me anymore, and then I found that cottage. The woman agreed to help when I gave her a half crown.'

'Ah yes.' Gareth fumbled in his waistcoat pocket and held up the coin. 'Your half crown! I traded it for a guinea, and a jug of milk that we tipped down your throat.'

'Thank you, my lord. I'm not sure if those people would have helped me. She went inside to get something for me to drink and then I must have fainted. I did not realize that a lack of water causes such havoc. I have never fainted before in my whole life. Mr Dantes and his friend have left?'

Gareth's eyes narrowed. His expression would have warned any of his acquaintances that they should be on their guard. 'Yes, he's bolted, but you can be sure there is a price on their heads as we have informed the law. I can only apologize that a member of my family was responsible for these awful deeds.'

'It is none of your fault, sir!'

He looked out of the carriage window for a moment. 'Perhaps not, but maybe it is in a roundabout way. I have never understood him. He had every advantage in life, but has ended up as a repugnant and morally depraved character. He knows just how much I dislike him.'

'I confess I did not fully understand at first why you hated him. It was obvious to me that you did every time I saw you together.'

Gareth laughed. 'Yes, that is true. It has never bothered me so much as it has lately that he is officially my heir until I have a son of my own.' He looked down at her. 'Enough talk! Close your eyes and try to rest. I am taking you straight to your aunt and uncle. You will mention what happened to them and no one else. You must also beg them to tell no other. That way there will be no damage to your reputation, or that of Miss Wilcox.'

Julia opened her mouth to reply, but he placed a well-manicured finger on her lips and she succumbed. She now knew with blinding certainty that she loved him. She loved his quiet art and the way he behaved. She respected his attitude and how he felt responsible for his family. She respected him because he was honest and likeable, when you knew him better. There would never be another moment for her like this.

They were alone in his carriage and her head was resting on his thigh. The jogging and jerking of the vehicle as it went along sent her to sleep. Her companion studied her indulgently, and thanked heaven that he had found her, before an appalling tragedy had happened. It didn't bear thinking about. At this moment, he could strangle Fenton with his bare hands if he was within reach.

When they arrived, the marquess left Julia to wait in the coach and got her worried aunt alone in her sitting room. He explained briefly what had happened, and that she should give Julia into the care of a servant she could trust and be kept away from any other curious servants until she was clean and properly dressed. Her present appearance would give rise to all kinds of speculation, but could be explained by her staying unexpectedly with her friend overnight.

Her aunt was overjoyed to hear Julia was unharmed. She called for Maggie, and sent the other servants about their business. Julia was spirited into the hall and up the stairs quickly to her room.

She had no time to say goodbye to Gareth or thank him. He left with a polite bow to her aunt and a fleeting glance at her as Maggie shepherded her up the stairs.

* * *

A day later, she was recovered enough to visit Amelia. They fell into each other's arms, each glad that the other had survived without harm. Hugh Grenville called as she was leaving. When she saw Hugh and Amelia together, Julia speculated whether she would hear news about them soon.

The season had little attraction for Julia anymore, and she decided to return home a few days earlier than planned. John called to see how she was faring, and when he heard she was leaving he offered to travel with her. 'I can see you safely home, and visit your mother before travelling on.'

'It is kind of you, John, but only if you are sure. I confess I did not fancy journeying on my own with strangers. I am sure Mama will love to see you, and you can break your journey and stay overnight with us. I will write to Mama today. Does it suit you if we travel on Friday?'

He nodded. 'Of course.' He paused before he said, 'You are perfectly well, I hope? It was quite damnable what those blackguards did. I expect you are a little nervous of strangers, but that will fade.'

Julia felt happier now that she had made definite plans. She did not hear from the marquess, but she hadn't expected to. A letter arrived from Mama that included another letter for her from a firm of solicitors. As she read it, her hand flew to her mouth. She sat staring at the words for quite a while before she dashed upstairs and found her aunt writing letters in her boudoir.

Handing her the letter, she said, 'Look what has just arrived! I can hardly believe it.'

Her aunt read it and whooped. 'Julia, how wonderful. Your papa *did* manage to tend to your future before he died, after all. Ten thousand pounds! It will ensure you a safe, comfortable living.'

Julia nodded. Her colour was high and her eyes sparkled. 'Have you noticed that he went to a new firm of solicitors to arrange it, so that the transaction would never be confused with estate affairs? The money came from his personal fortune so that cousin Henry can never contest its source.'

Julia thought with pleasure of the security and independence her papa had arranged for her. 'It seems that these lawyers were unaware that he had died, until they tried to contact him recently about the interest the settlement had earned since he arranged it.'

Her aunt got up and hugged her. 'I am so delighted for you, my dear. It will make all the difference. I will not worry about you quite as much now.'

Julia laughed and hugged her back.

* * *

Friday morning came faster than Julia expected. She barely had time to buy the presents she wanted for Mama, George and May. She said her goodbyes to any acquaintances she happened to meet, and packed her bags. Her aunt had persuaded her to travel post-chaise instead of by stagecoach. She reminded Julia that she could now afford this little luxury, and John also declared it was an excellent idea.

They left London early on Friday. Julia said her farewell to her aunt and uncle with profuse thanks, carrying loving messages home for her mother. The post-chaise made good time, stopping only once for refreshments of bacon and ham and fresh bread at an inn with a rousing fire. The establishment was a picture of convenience and neatness. Julia appreciated it because she recalled her journey to London, when the stagecoach had also stopped at an inn for fresh horses; but it had been a dirty, uncomfortable place. The bread was salty and bitter, and a single glass of wine was inordinately dear. There had been a scramble for coffee and ham for breakfast. When they'd stopped and she'd looked around, Julia had foregone the food and spent the time watching the men changing the horses.

Even the post-chaise had to pick its way through rutty lanes, but the carriage was more comfortable and not so full. A few hours later it set them down with their bags almost outside her mother's cottage, and the door flew open as they walked up the path. It was only seconds before Julia was in her mother's arms.

The following day was one of pleasure. Her mother had her daughter back, and a friend of her son's had called to see her. They spent time reminiscing and chatting. John already knew about how Julia's father had settled money on her, and it was a pleasure for her to tell her mother what was in the letter from the solicitors. Lady Stratton could hardly believe it, but she was almost more delighted than her daughter. She knew how much difference it would make, and it reduced the worry that was always at the back of their minds.

Julia held back the news about the attempted abduction to herself until John had left and was on his way to visit his parents. He didn't mention it, and understood that Julia needed the right moment to tell her mother all that had happened. He promised that he would call again as soon as time and his army service allowed. Julia liked him, and not just because he'd been her brother's friend. He was a kind and generous man; and even if his profession was rough, he had retained all that was good in a gentleman. If she had been as observant as her mother, she would have noted there was more than just a look of regret in his expression as he left.

Her mother was shocked beyond belief, and then enraged about what might have happened if Amelia and Julia hadn't escaped in time. She regained some of her calm and patted her daughter's knee.

'You are well, Julia? I hope that dreadful man really did not hurt you in any way?'

Julia shook her head violently. 'No, no! We both got away in time. I shudder to think what could have happened, but I am trying to forget it all now.'

Her mother nodded. 'Now you are back in your home, you will soon settle down again, I'm sure.'

10

Julia didn't accompany her mother to church the next morning. She declared she needed a little time for herself. Her mother understood and set off as usual. Julia had forgotten to tell her not to mention Fenton Dantes to anyone else. When she asked her mother if she'd mentioned it, she said, 'I didn't think you would mind if I told Maria, but don't worry, she would never gossip about us. She is my friend as well as the wife of our vicar.'

Julia was glad to set about tidying the garden again on Monday. It diverted her thoughts and gave her something sensible to do. The garden looked well, but her absence had made a difference, and there were plenty of weeds and dead flowers flourishing between all the prettiness — even though George had kept the weeds at bay among the vegetables. She enjoyed the feeling of being at home, and how her mother, George and May, appreciated her gifts. They all insisted they had missed her. London was exciting, but she'd had enough excitement for a while. Her father's settlement would now enable her to sleep without worries. The future looked a lot brighter.

That afternoon, she was having tea with her mother as usual when May entered and announced that they had a visitor. She moved to the side, and the Lady de Vere entered in a flurry of lilac silk. Julia and her mother were so surprised that they almost forgot to rise and curtsey.

'Forgive me for calling unannounced like this, Lady Stratton, but I just called to see Mrs Dutton with a contribution towards the school fund. She mentioned that your daughter was back from London, and as we met her there, I thought I'd call and ask if her journey was uneventful. Mrs Dutton said she travelled in a post-chaise. It was probably most uncomfortable, and all sorts of mishaps can occur between here and London. A private coach would have been better.' She looked at Julia. 'You are somewhat paler than when we first met, but then in London you were not able to spend much time in the garden, were you?'

Julia laughed softly. 'No, that is very true, your ladyship. My aunt has no garden to speak of. Just a strip of green at the back of the house.'

Julia's mother gestured to the china and dish of small cakes. 'May we offer you tea, your ladyship? I will get our maid to brew a fresh pot.'

'Do that, Lady Stratton. And in the meantime your daughter can show me her garden.' She turned away, and Julia had no alternative but to follow her through the hall and outside. She managed to talk about the patch of garden directly in front of the house for a few minutes before offering to show her the vegetable patch. Julia was not sure that she was even listening to what she was saying. When they reached the corner of the cottage, Lady de Vere stopped and turned to face her.

'Miss Stratton, I only used the garden as an excuse to get you alone and ask your forgiveness that a member of my family has subjected you to such an ordeal. I must admit that Mrs Dutton was not the first person to tell me of what happened.'

Julia stiffened. 'My mother asked Mrs Dutton not to broadcast it any further. I did not think she would gossip.'

'Do not blame the woman. I called on her this morning by chance and, as I knew she and your mother are friends, I tricked her into admitting she'd heard of it from your mother. I think she only conceded because she fears me a little. She was quite upset and close to tears when she realized she'd given things away. I had to keep reassuring her that no one else would hear of it from me and she should also keep it secret. I'm sure she will do so. She does not seem to know of the connection between the de Vere family and Fenton Dantes. You can be sure I have absolutely no reason to want to have it spread abroad. My son called at Cobham before leaving for Devon on business and told me what had happened. I have rarely seen him in such a temper. He is usually a very calm and collected character. It was a terrible thing for anyone to do.'

Julia's colour heightened. 'Then you will also know that your son found me and rescued me. I must have looked simply dreadful, and I was so dirty I probably ruined his coach or his clothing. It was not your fault, your ladyship, nor anyone else's in your family. Most families have a black sheep, and I'm afraid Fenton Dantes is yours.'

'I shudder to think what will happen to the estate if any harm comes to Gareth.'

Julia wrung her hands and studied the tips of her shoes peeping out from beneath the hem of her dress. 'You can be certain that I will pray that never happens, ma'am.'

'If Fenton was capable of trying to abduct you with the very worst of intentions, he's capable of anything. It's a scandal and doesn't bear thinking about.' She held Julia's glance. 'I am sure he is capable of trying to murder my son, or paying someone else to do it for him.'

Julia paled at the thought. 'He wouldn't dare, would he?'

Lady de Vere's lips thinned. 'Fenton is evil. He always was malicious, and the older he became the more depraved and debauched he grew too. I don't understand why he is like he is. His mother is a gentle soul, but she has never had any control over him. His father died years ago. He was also a bit of a rake, but as far as I know he didn't have the kind of evil, immoral standards Fenton has.'

'Then I hope that he will stay on the continent for the rest of his life. I heard him say he was going to France. I can't imagine why he picked on my friend and me, as neither of us is very rich.'

'Who knows? But I can guess why. Thank heavens you managed to thwart his intentions. I don't think there are many women of your age who would have been so courageous or inventive. You outwitted him.'

Julia laughed. 'I was lucky. If he hadn't accepted my bargain to let my friend Amelia go, I wouldn't have had a chance. He was too strong for me to fight him, and Amelia would never have managed to climb down the wall of the house via the ivy like I did.'

Lady de Vere's lips twitched. 'To be honest, when I think about it, I don't believe there are many ladies of my acquaintance who could have managed that either.' She straightened. 'I came to see you and also to invite you to visit Cobham, to share tea with me as my way of apology, and perhaps we can stroll around our vegetable garden together. I can't recall ever doing so, but there is a first time for everything in this life.'

Julia knew she should not refuse, but she tried. She wanted to forget the de Vere family. There was no reason that she or her mother would ever receive another invitation. The invitation to the picnic had been a concealed way of saying thank you for helping the marquess. She needed time to distance herself, and to steel herself to hearing the news that he was to be married. It hurt that he would never know she loved him, but it could never be.

'Please don't believe you are obliged to invite me, ma'am, because of what's happened. It was an unpleasant episode, but it is over. Your son helped me, so things are levelled out between us. I will be grateful if everyone forgets it and never refers to it again.'

Lady de Vere brushed her words aside. 'Wednesday, three-thirty! Now we will return indoors, and I am sure your mother has a decent pot of tea ready and waiting. I'll try one of those little cakes. They look quite delicious.' She turned back to the entrance and

Julia had no other choice but to follow. The two older women chatted quite amiably, and Lady de Vere even complimented Julia's mother on how comfortable and ladylike the rooms in the cottage were.

* * *

Wednesday loomed, and Julia's thoughts were lightened when a letter arrived from Amelia.

My dear Julia,

You are reading some hurried lines that come from the happiest girl in the world. Hugh has asked for my hand, and my parents have agreed.

I think you already realize that I've had a tendre for him ever since we met, but I did not dare to hope that he felt the same. It is so exciting, and I feel like I am drifting on a cloud of happiness. We are to travel to meet Hugh's family next weekend. His parents have invited us to their home and have assured me in a very kind letter that they welcome the news and look forward to meeting me, and my parents. Mama is already dreadfully nervous, even more nervous than I am myself!

I am of course not sure if Hugh's parents perhaps hoped for a better match for their son, but Hugh tells me that if he had been given the choice between marrying a princess of the royal blood or me, I would always win straight off. Isn't that romantic? He has talked of his house in Berkshire and says it is badly in need of a woman's touch. I am sure I will enjoy being its mistress and making a home with him there. Perhaps you can find the time to come on a visit and make suggestions? You have such good taste. I think Hugh and I will do well together.

I know that you like Hugh, so I am sure that I will receive your blessing. I just hope that one day you will find someone just as good and will be just as happy. As you have always alleged you will never marry, this seems unlikely, but we will always be friends whatever happens. I will never forget how you were prepared to sacrifice yourself to that horrible man in order to give me the chance to escape.

I must close now. Hugh will be here soon, and we are going for a walk in the park together. I am sure he would send his love if he knew I was writing to you. He has told me several times how much he likes you! We will probably set the date for our marriage before Christmas, and I insist that you must be my bridesmaid.

Write back soon,
Love
Amelia

Julia felt a glow and was happy for them both. They were well suited.

Amelia's parents would jump at the chance of seeing their daughter so well settled.

She'd personally liked Hugh from the moment they'd met. It had taken a little longer for her to like the marquess, but 'like' was the wrong word now. She liked Hugh; she loved Gareth.

Julia hurried downstairs and handed her letter to her mother.

'What splendid news! Her parents will be delighted. Amelia was always a good girl. I hope the two of them will be very happy. Mr Grenville seems to be a real gentleman. I remember how much I liked him when he called with the marquess that day. You must reply at once, and send her my congratulations and my love.' The mention of the marquess reminded her of Julia's invitation. She looked at the clock. 'Julia! You must get ready. Don't keep the Lady de Vere waiting. What are you going to wear?'

Julia didn't really care what she wore, but she wanted to humour her mother.

'The eau de Nil with the embroidered edging round the neck and the hem?'

Her mother nodded her approval. 'Smart but not ostentatious. Wear your chip bonnet with it, and your paisley shawl. You'd better wear your soft brown half-boots because of driving there.'

* * *

An hour later, Julia was on her way. Peggy trotted at a good pace, and Julia enjoyed the feeling of independence and the wind on her face. She turned in through the wrought-iron gates and down the long track that led to the house. Stopping in front of the entrance steps, she stepped down and admired the façade. It was well proportioned, and she liked the colour of the stonework. The butler came down the steps and welcomed her with exquisite courtesy. He motioned to another servant in livery to take the pony and cart.

'Good afternoon, Miss Stratton. Lady

de Vere is expecting you. Follow me, please.'

Julia hitched her dress, climbed the steps and went inside. The entrance hall was as grand as she'd expected, with black and white tiling, a wide staircase that led to the upper rooms, and ancient statues that stood in niches around the walls. As she had just come from London and attended so many events in stately homes, the immediate effect of Cobham's grandness was dampened slightly, but she was still very impressed. She followed the butler until he knocked on a door, opened it, and announced her name.

Lady de Vere was seated on an uncomfortable-looking sofa. She got up and came towards Julia. 'You are punctual. That is good. I am glad you came. I was afraid you might not.'

Julia laughed softly. 'I was afraid to refuse. Was it obvious that I wasn't very eager to comply, your ladyship?'

'I'm very skilled at reading people's reactions, and you weren't exactly delighted when I issued the invitation.'

'I was surprised because, as I told you at the time, there was no reason for you to do so.'

'Sit down.' She gestured to a chair nearby. 'I invited you because I like you. I like your spirit, and you have been well brought up.'

'That is thanks to my parents.'

'And your character!'

The butler returned with a maid in tow carrying a tray with crockery and a coffee pot. 'Shall I serve, madam?'

'No, Thomas,' she dismissed him. 'We will manage very well on our own.' He bowed and left. 'Pour us some coffee, child, and take one of those cakes if you will. The ones your mother offered taste much better. She must give me the recipe one day.'

Julia poured two cups, added sugar to her own, registered how Lady de Vere shook her head, and handed her the plain cup of coffee. She picked up her cup and took a sip. 'Um! Coffee is a luxury we only drink on special days.

This is very good.'

'I heard that you have come into a settlement from your father?'

Julia was startled. 'How do you know about that?'

Lady de Vere gave one of her rare smiles. 'It is the privilege of an ex-marchioness to have access to information about someone, once their name is mentioned in the right circles.'

'It sounds more like someone running their own secret service. You would consider my settlement to be mere pin-money, but it will make all the difference to my life.'

Lady de Vere's smile flickered, and she stared at Julia for a moment before she burst out laughing. 'You will do! Indeed you will do! Not many people would dare to suggest that I pry and snoop for information.'

'I didn't intend to be rude, ma'am. But I find it rather strange. We are not connected and we live in different worlds. Why am I of interest?'

'It will all be explained shortly. What

do you think of Cobham?'

'Impressive, well designed and well cared for. I haven't seen much of the inside, but what I have seen is striking.'

She nodded. 'All of the estates need constant care. Gareth is always travelling between all of them. I like Cobham and have decided to remain here in the Dower House. When and if Gareth marries, of course his wife will have the final say in everything, otherwise she will never be properly respected. It will be a bonus for me if I see grandchildren growing up here at Cobham. I only see my daughter's children a couple of times a year.'

Julia swallowed a lump in her throat. 'Does the marquess intend to marry in the near future, your ladyship?'

She shrugged. 'I am not yet absolutely certain. I would greet it, but my son is a very private person and generally he does not inform me of his intentions in advance. Like his father, he knows when to look for support and when to carry his own decisions. I have an inkling that he is thinking strongly of marriage at present.'

Julia looked down into her empty cup and remained silent.

'Have you heard that Hugh Grenville is to marry? I can't recall what the girl looks like, although she was present at that assembly in London with you when we met. Hugh will have chosen well, I have no doubt of that.'

'I received the news this morning, and I am very pleased for them both. I think they are well suited.'

'I wondered at one time if Hugh and you . . . '

Honestly surprised, Julia uttered, 'Hugh is a very nice person and a gentleman, but I have never thought of him in any other way than as a friend, and I'm sure he considers me a friend and nothing more either.'

Lady de Vere nodded. 'As I thought! Shall we take a walk and view the vegetable garden? I imagine you will be very interested. The gardeners have already been informed that my visitor has a small vegetable plot of her own. Apparently they are looking forward to meeting someone at last who appreciates and understands their work.'

Julia got up and placed her cup on the tray. Once they had toured the kitchen garden, she would be able to make a departure. 'Gladly, ma'am. Perhaps you will lead the way?'

The kitchen garden was walled. The head gardener was waiting at the entrance with his cap in his hands. He dipped his head as they approached. 'Your ladyship! Miss!'

Lady de Vere declared, 'Benson, this is the young lady I was telling you about, the one who likes gardening.'

He nodded at Julia. 'If you will follow me, miss. Is there anything in particular you would like to see?'

'No.' She looked around. 'Everything looks in an excellent state of care. Much superior to my little patch, and you have room for a greater variety of vegetables. What a wonderful latticework with peaches along the wall!'

'That wall gets most of the sun in the summer, and the peach trees seem to love it.'

Fascinated, Julia said, 'I would love to have some fruit trees, but apart from one apple tree in the corner, I have no space. We need the vegetables more than fruit. At the moment our onions are not looking good. Are you having any difficulties with them, Mr Benson?'

Soon they were deep in conversation about blight and snails and other pests. Lady de Vere looked on and wondered why anyone should be interested in such things, especially a young lady with looks and brains like Julia. She checked her fob watch. 'I have forgotten to inform my maid that I will need my cashmere shawl this evening and she must take it out for airing. I will leave you for a moment, Miss Stratton. You are in good hands.'

Julia looked at her. 'If you wish, I will go back and inform one of the servants to tell your maid so. It will only take me a couple of minutes.'

She brushed her words aside. 'You carry on here. If your conversation with Benson is merely about various garden bugs and diseases, I assure you that I will not miss a thing. I will see you shortly.' She turned and headed for the entrance arch.

11

Julia returned her attention to what the gardener was pointing out. She was slightly envious. The rows of vegetable were in prime condition. Her little patch at home was nothing in comparison.

She was following the gardener to take a closer look at the cold frame containing some pumpkins when a movement at the entrance caught her eye. Marquess de Vere strode determinedly towards them. Julia was glad of the few seconds she had to bury her astonishment. His mother had not mentioned he was at home. Indeed, during their conversation she left Julia with the impression that he was away on business. She hoped that the colour she felt flooding her cheeks would recede before he reached her. The gardener tipped his cap dutifully.

Gareth nodded to him. 'I'd like a

private word with Miss Stratton. Can you find something else to do?'

'Of course, my lord. I'll disappear for a while.' He withdrew in the direction from which the marquess had come.

Gareth bowed slightly to Julia and held out his hand. She bobbed and accepted it for a second. It felt warm and pleasant. His smile hovered. He stared at her with knitted brows.

She felt tongue-tied but she made an effort. 'Good afternoon, your lordship. I did not realize you were at home. Your mother invited me to tea.'

He nodded. 'I know.'

Her voice sounded strange, even to her own ears. 'I never had the chance to thank you for finding me that day and taking me back to my aunt. We didn't see each other in London after that.' She was rooted to the ground like any of the nearby vegetables. She wondered how to escape. Just being this close to him robbed her of air.

'Don't mention that day to me.' He said in a dangerously calm voice, 'I have never felt so helpless and angry. I guessed why Fenton did it and why he chose you and your friend. He has done his best to annoy me often in recent years, and he knew I was acquainted with you and Miss Wilcox. It is the kind of thing he enjoys planning just to madden me. He was very successful that day, if that was his aim.' He paused for a moment and his eyes watched her closely. 'You have heard that Hugh and your friend are betrothed?'

With a dry throat she replied, 'Yes; it is good news. Or do you think it is not an appropriate union?'

He shrugged impatiently. 'It's not my job to decide if it is appropriate or not. I trust in Hugh's judgement. I hope they are well suited and I wish them happiness. You don't mind?'

Startled, she uttered, 'Mind? Why should I mind? Amelia is a dear friend, and I hope Hugh is my friend too.'

Gareth said promptly, 'I wondered for some time if you and he would be more than friends one day. From the time we met here until later in London, I was never sure which one of you Hugh liked more. He was always high in his praise of you, as well as of your friend. I trod carefully and didn't ask too many questions until I was certain where his interest had fallen. I didn't want to stand in the way of your happiness, if that was how things were to end.'

Puzzled but then answering in a voice bordering on alarm, she replied, 'I never thought of Hugh as more than a friend, sir! I liked him as soon as I met him. But I also suspected that he liked my friend even more. He is like the kind of brother I don't have anymore. I hoped that they would grow to love each other, but I never questioned either of them. I left it up to fate.'

'Then you are free to consider my offer?'

'Your offer? Forgive me, sir, but what are you talking about? What offer?'

'I am offering for your hand.'

If Julia had felt surprise and alarm at

seeing him so suddenly, she now felt a shockwave. 'Don't be silly, my lord! You don't want to marry me. You are perfectly aware that my situation is unsuitable. I am socially below you, and I am too bold and audacious. I am totally unfitting.' Her voice broke a little and she stammered, 'It is an honour that you offer, whatever your motive might be, but it won't do. I have no thought of marriage to anyone, ever.'

'I wish you would stop calling me 'my lord'. My name is Gareth, as you well know. You also know me well enough to agree that I am not always good, and I am not always kind either! But you can make a better man of me, and I am certain a marriage to you would never be boring. That is a great attraction. By now Hugh has figured out what a fix I am in; he knows how much I liked you, and how that liking has turned into love. He also knows that I am likely to botch my declaration about how I feel.' His expression moved smoothly from one of hesitation to one of hopeful expectancy. Julia longed to touch his face. 'I cannot, I repeat I cannot, face the mortification of being rejected and having to tell Hugh I was hare-brained and couldn't convince you.'

'I am sensible of the honour, but you know yourself that such an idea . . . is sheer madness. Can you imagine what society, what your mother, would think about such an unsuitable match?'

'My dear lady, do you honestly think that I care what she or anyone else thinks or says? Don't talk such nonsense! I may have acted like an arrogant fool sometimes when we met, but I have since learned that etiquette and living by the rules of society will not make me happy. Stop worrying! Your family is perfectly acceptable. Look at mine and its felonious offshoots. I am asking for your hand in marriage. I want you at my side. If you don't agree, I swear that I will marry no other, and then you alone will be responsible for Fenton inheriting everything.'

She spluttered, 'Stop it! Do not try to

blackmail me, sir!'

He laughed indulgently. 'I expected you to react so.'

'You are not in love with me. How could you be? I am outspoken, frank and used to speaking my mind. These are not the qualities you need in a wife.'

He ran his hand over his face. 'Lord, give me strength! I know exactly how you are. I have been watching you ever since that fortunate day when I had an accident outside you mother's cottage. It is just because of how you are, how you act and react that I love you. There are too many colourless, simpering, timid creatures to be had everywhere. I fell in love with you, and if you refuse me, I will be miserable thereafter. I will never be happy unless I have you there with me.' He took a step forward and took her ruthlessly in his arms.

'Oh . . . ' She gasped for air as she emerged from his kiss and his embrace. Looking up into his smiling face, she said unsteadily, 'You really mean it, don't you?'

A light burned in the depth of his dark eyes. 'I have never been so serious. If you say you do not love me, I will have to live with it, but it will not stop me loving you.' He possessed her hands and held them firmly.

Julia couldn't believe this was happening, but she loved him too much to lie. She said shyly, 'I do love you, Gareth. Not because of what you stand for and your possessions, but because of who you are. Behind your mask of indifference there is a man of great quality. You are someone I can love and respect. I found out weeks ago that I am only really happy when you are near me.'

'That is all I want to hear. You accept? You agree to be my wife?'

'Yes — how can I refuse you?'

He bent and kissed her again. She was trembling and her brain was in a whirl. He held her at arm's length for a moment and said, 'At last! I must speak with your mother and get her permission straight away. Strictly speaking, I should have asked her first.'

With pink cheeks and shiny eyes, she remarked, 'Mama will be quite shocked. I don't think she has ever given you more than a passing thought. I was careful not to talk about you, and I only ever mentioned your name casually whenever I wrote from London. I did not want her to know I loved someone in vain. I did not want to give myself away.'

He eyed her silently for a moment. 'That means you have loved me for a while too?'

She nodded. He threw his arm around her shoulders and kissed her cheek. 'Come — we will begin our duties together. We'll tell my mother and then seek your mother's blessing.'

When they reached the entrance to the kitchen garden, Benson was waiting. Gareth waved him away. 'Miss Stratton has no more time today, Benson, but I can assure you that she will soon have plenty of time to examine and discuss matters to do with the cabbages and onions and anything else growing in this place.' Looking a little puzzled, the man tipped the brim of his hat and turned away.

Gareth looked at her. 'I just realized something. Women are generally very romantic creatures. I hope you will never censure me, or constantly remind me, that I proposed to you in the middle of a vegetable garden!'

She squeezed his hand and laughed. 'I promise that I won't. I love vegetable gardens.'

'Oh . . . ' He came to a sudden stop. 'I didn't provide myself with a suitable ring either. I told myself that it might bring me bad luck. We will choose something suitable from the family jewellery and have it put into the kind of setting you like. I do have something else that I hope you will like, though.' He reached into his pocket and drew out a silver chain with a half-crown medallion.

'The half crown you gave me in the garden, the one I gave that woman later?'

'Yes.'

Julia reached up and kissed his cheek. He slipped it over her head and kissed her lips. 'Thank you, Gareth. I will never own anything that means more to me than this.'

They were still standing, lost between themselves, when footfalls on the gravel dragged them back to the present. It was Lady de Vere. She looked sternly from one to the other. Losing no time, and taking the initiative, Gareth said, 'Mama, I have just asked Miss Stratton to be my wife, and she has done me the honour of accepting.'

Julia drew a deep breath and met her glance. For a moment there was unadulterated silence. 'Miss Stratton, I have waited several years for my son to present me with a suitable bride, and now he has chosen you.'

Julia straightened her back and was glad to feel the support of Gareth's arm around her shoulder. His mother took another step forward and they were face to face.

'I have sometimes argued about decisions he has made, but I am in full agreement with this one. I cannot think of anyone who is more suitable to become the new Marchioness de Vere. Welcome to the family, my dear!'

Julia was immensely relieved, even if her knees felt like jelly. 'Thank you, your ladyship. I will try to be worthy of the title, and I hope I can always depend on you for advice and assistance.'

The older woman took her in her arms and kissed her on the cheek. 'You can depend on that, but I have the feeling you will have little need of it. I will fill my time doing good deeds and visiting the poor of the parish. Perhaps I can involve myself in that school you were hoping to establish. Come! Let us go inside where we can toast your happiness. I am sure the rest of the family will do the same when they hear.'

* * *

That evening when she was preparing for bed, Julia could not believe than anyone could be happier.

Her mother had been duly surprised and shocked by the news, but when she looked at her daughter's face it was clear to her that it was a love match, and that was more than just pleasing. A few weeks ago Julia was certain that nothing would entice her to marry, and now she had agreed to marry a man who clearly loved her and would give her the kind of life her mother had always hoped she would have one day. Lady Stratton already liked him. She would have liked him if he hadn't had a title, but it did nothing to distract from his attraction either. She gave her permission gladly, and accepted his invitation to come to Cobham for lunch with the family on the morrow.

Julia was too excited to sleep, so instead she sat down to write a letter to her friend.

Dear Amelia,

I have already sent you my best wishes, and love, on the occasion of your engagement to Hugh.

Now, in return, I am asking for yours. Gareth has asked me to marry him and I have accepted. I am extremely happy and have yet to come back down to earth. I can now admit that I have loved him for some time. I think I was successful at concealing it from you and the world in general, wasn't I? I didn't have an inkling that he loved me too, so you see we were at cross purposes because he was just as ingenious as I was at hiding the truth — even from Hugh until recently.

I feel just a little nervous when I think of the task that faces me when I am at his side, but I know I will always have his support and that of everyone else that I love. I hope to use any influence I gain to improve the situation for those who are not as fortunate as I am. Gareth knows that, and supports me wholeheartedly.

Write to me soon. I send my best wishes to your Hugh. I expect he will hear from Gareth in due course. That is also so delightful. Your future husband and mine have always been friends, just as you and I have been friends since our childhood. It will strengthen our joint alliances even more.

Love,
Julia

We do hope that you have enjoyed reading this large print book.

Did you know that all of our titles are available for purchase?

We publish a wide range of high quality large print books including:
Romances, Mysteries, Classics
General Fiction
Non Fiction and Westerns

Special interest titles available in large print are:
The Little Oxford Dictionary
Music Book, Song Book
Hymn Book, Service Book

Also available from us courtesy of Oxford University Press:
Young Readers' Dictionary (large print edition)
Young Readers' Thesaurus (large print edition)

For further information or a free brochure, please contact us at:

Ulverscroft Large Print Books Ltd., The Green, Bradgate Road, Anstey, Leicester, LE7 7FU, England.
Tel: (00 44) **0116 236 4325**
Fax: (00 44) **0116 234 0205**

Other titles in the
Linford Romance Library:

THE MOST WONDERFUL TIME OF THE YEAR

Wendy Kremer

After ditching her cheating boyfriend, Sara escapes to a small village for Christmas, expecting to find rest and relaxation without the usual seasonal stresses. But her landlady, Emma, soon involves her in the village's holiday preparations, and the magic of Christmas begins to weave its spell. While Sara settles in and makes new friends, she also relishes the special attentions of Emma's handsome neighbour, Alex, and his young daughter. Could she actually have a future here — and is this Christmas destined to be her best ever?